THE
DESERT RIDER

Center Point
Large Print

Also by L. P. Holmes and available from
Center Point Large Print:

The Crimson Hills
Free Winds Blow West
Orphans of Gunswift Graze
The Sunset Trail
Once in the Saddle
Doom Patrol

**This Large Print Book carries the
Seal of Approval of N.A.V.H.**

THE
DESERT
RIDER

L. P. Holmes

CENTER POINT LARGE PRINT
THORNDIKE, MAINE

This Circle Ⓥ Western is published by
Center Point Large Print in the year 2019 in
co-operation with Golden West Literary Agency.

May 2019
First Edition

Printed in the United States of America
on permanent paper.
Set in 16-point Times New Roman type.

ISBN: 978-1-64358-201-6

Library of Congress Cataloging-in-Publication Data

Names: Holmes, L. P. (Llewellyn Perry), 1895-1988, author.
Title: The desert rider : a western duo / L.P. Holmes.
Description: First Edition. | Thorndike, Maine : Center Point Large Print,
    2019. | Series: A Circle V Western
Identifiers: LCCN 2019005246 | ISBN 9781643582016 (hardcover :
    alk. paper)
Classification: LCC PS3515.O4448 D472 2019 | DDC 813/.52—dc23
LC record available at https://lccn.loc.gov/2019005246

BLACK ROCK DESERT

I

The horse herd broke and began its run right after topping the crest of the pass. It was what Lee Cone had been afraid would happen, and he had warned Braz Boland to that effect during the brief noon stop in the desert, suggesting that the herd be held over for the night on the south side of the pass, and the crossing made the next morning.

It was advice Boland had waved aside. He wasn't, he declared, spending another thirsty night in the desert. Boland had added a further caustic remark to the effect that he had hired Lee on at Carbide Junction for just two things. One was to show him the shortest way across the desert; the other was to chouse horses. Then he had ordered Lee to get up at point and to hold the herd back if it began to get restless.

Lee hadn't argued the point. During the drive in across Black Rock Desert from Carbide Junction, he had achieved a deepening dislike of heavy-handed, sarcastic Braz Boland. But in another twenty-four hours the drive would be finished and he'd be paid off. That would be the time to tell Boland a thing or two and get it all off his chest.

• • •

It was full dark by the time the horse herd reached the crest of Smoky Pass. Up at point, Lee rode wearily, alert for the first sign of change in the weary shuffling of the massed hoofs behind him.

There was no change until the first sweep of the night wind, snaking through the pass from Maacama Basin beyond, brought with it the moist breath of the river. That did it. There was a gusty snorting, then a quickening roll of hoofs which almost instantly lifted to a battering roar.

It would be hopeless for any single rider to try to hold back this frenzied torrent. But Lee Cone did try. He drove his mount at the charging leaders of the herd. He yelled at them, beat at them with the hard coils of his riata. It was like trying to hold back an avalanche with a twig. Lee's horse was buffeted, spun around, and nearly knocked off its feet. So, bleakly understanding the danger of having his horse go down in front of all those wild hoofs, he gave the animal free rein and raced out ahead of it all.

Lee's first thought was that he would swing gradually to one side and thus angle into the clear, but he found this wouldn't do, either. For, free of the confines of the pass, the herd spread out on either hand, and a collision from the side would roll him and his horse under even more surely than any other way. There was nothing to do but race straight ahead as far as the river flats, where the thirst-crazed herd would break and spread and leave a man clear of danger.

The down sweep of the slope from this northern end of the pass to the river was a broad, gradually curving swale, with its sharpest turn situated just before it melted into the river flats. This swale held the racing herd as it would a torrent of water and, though the pace of the herd before the break had been slow and weary, now that it was running full out, the distance to the river flats shortened swiftly. And it was just as Lee Cone broke into the final turn of the swale that he saw the ruddy glow of a campfire, dead ahead.

He saw other things. He saw the dark loom of a heavy wagon at one fringe of the firelight glow, then the lift of tent flap to the other side. He saw human figures dodging this way and that away from the fire and toward the safety of the wagon. He could hear a man's voice calling desperately.

"Kip . . . Kip!"

Lee saw a dart of movement break from the tent, a slim, feminine figure, at the farthest reach of the firelight's thin radiance. Then he was certain as he made out a fluttering about her, perhaps a dress or a nightgown, as she ran, and he got the impression of pale hair flowing over her shoulders.

It needed only a glance to see that she'd never make the shelter of the wagon. She'd be caught in that short open interval. She'd be knocked down, trampled by the hoofs of the animals.

Lee hauled at his reins, drove straight at her, and hauled at the reins again, setting his horse up in a sliding, spinning half halt just short of her. He leaned far out from his saddle, swinging his right arm in a curve, yelling at her as he did so: "Grab! Grab at me!"

She had courage, this girl, and quickness of mind. She threw herself upward at Lee, into the circle of his reaching arm, her hands catching at his shoulders.

Lee had only enough time to haul her in against his hip when, from behind, frantic, thundering horseflesh crashed into his mount.

The impact drove them yards ahead, and for one bleak, heart-stopping moment, Lee was certain they were going down—his horse, himself, and this shaking, clinging girl. They did go half down, and this gave Lee the chance to lift the girl a little higher, to pull her closer and more securely to him. Then his floundering mount, fighting gallantly, found its feet again, surged and plunged madly, and broke suddenly into the small, clear eddy of safety in the lee of the wagon. For just at that instant the racing horse herd, as the big wagon loomed in its way, split like water around a rock, flowing around either side and belting its way on to the river.

The fire and the tent offered no similar areas of safety. A herd animal, hesitating and slowing at the fire flames in front of it, was smashed into by one of its fellows and driven skidding through, scattering coals and embers in all directions, and these in turn were trampled to nothingness by the wild hoofs pouring past. The tent was no obstacle at all, beaten down, flattened, torn, and shredded in an instant.

A horse struck the low, extended tongue of the wagon, turned completely over, came down in a thudding fall and lay as it fell, its head twisted under. Another animal, tripping over the same obstacle, went down, rolled, regained its feet, and blundered on, a front leg loose and swinging.

And then, abruptly, the last stragglers of the herd were past and gone, and the night lay breathless and numbed.

Figures crawled out from under the wagon.

A woman's voice lifted, thin and strained with fright. "Kip! Kip child!"

"I'm all right, Mother."

The voice, slightly husky, and with only the slightest of tremors in it, was so close to Lee Cone's ear he could feel the faint breath. And now it was to him she spoke.

"You're holding me so tight I . . . I can hardly breathe."

Lee let the pressure of his arm relax and she slid out of his grasp and away from him to the ground.

He spoke gruffly. "Sorry. I just wanted to make

11

sure I didn't drop you, once I had hold of you."

There was a childish whimpering coming from beneath the wagon, and then again the woman's thin, strained voice.

"Kip . . . you're sure you're all right?" she asked as she moved toward the wagon.

"Yes, Mother. I'm sure I'm quite all right. Everything is all right now."

Lee Cone stepped from his saddle, held to his saddle horn, for his knees felt too rubbery to keep him upright. It had been a close encounter, and the aftereffects were working through his body.

Suddenly a man came out of the dark, angry and truculent.

"What the devil's the idea, running horses wild and crazy through the night like that through our camp? You might have killed me and my whole family!"

Lee let out a long, slow breath. "Sorry about it, friend. It was one of those things. Me and a couple of others brought that horse herd in across the Black Rock Desert for Braz Boland. The herd was in desperate need for water, and when they got the scent of the river, they broke and ran straight for it. I was riding point, but there was nothing I could do to hold them back. Too bad your camp happened to be in the way."

"Why shouldn't my camp be here?" came the harsh retort. "This is my land. I settled on it. I got a right to camp. . . ."

Then: "Dad . . . please!"

It was the girl, in that same rich slightly husky voice. "He had no way of knowing we'd be camped here. Let's all be thankful it came out as well as it did. Instead of blaming him, I think we should thank the man for doing what he did . . . especially for me." Her hand dropped easily on Lee's arm. "I do thank you, greatly," she said, looking away from her father and up at Lee.

"The luck broke good . . . for both of us," Lee told her simply.

Now came the pound of more hoofs, racing down from the pass. And in the midst of that pounding ahead Braz Boland's heavy shout was carried.

"Cone! Where the hell are you? Cone!"

Lee moved out and past the end of the wagon and sent his answer. "Over here!"

They came racing up, Boland and Jack Dhu. They pulled in by the dark loom of the wagon and Boland's voice ran profane and wild as his eyes bored into the darkness and settled on Lee.

"What in hell are you doing here? Why ain't you with the horses? What did you let them get away from you for? Damned if I ain't got the notion . . ."

"Cut it fine, Boland . . . cut it fine!" Lee's voice hit back curtly. "And watch your language, there are women here. The herd stampeded right through this camp and we're lucky that nobody was trampled."

"To hell with the camp!" fumed Boland. "My horse herd is all I'm interested in! And only a lunk-headed, sod-busting granger would be dumb enough to set up a camp right here. . . ."

Now it was the man of the camp who cut in.

"And what kind of a fool would try and bring a herd of horses through that pass at night, after bringing them in across the desert? You might have known the animals would be crazy for water and that they'd break and run as soon as they smelled the river. You own the herd?"

"I do, granger," snapped Boland. "What about it?"

"This about it," was the sturdy reply. "You've caused me damage, and I expect you to make good. I'm John Vail. What's your name?"

In the short silence that fell, Lee Cone could sense sly retreat on the part of Boland. Mention of a possible damage claim stilled some of the bluster in him. Lee's steadily accumulating dislike of the man now deepened into pure contempt.

He stepped back into his saddle and lifted his voice clearly. "You must have missed it when I mentioned the name of the owner of the herd before, friend. It's Boland . . . Braz Boland. Me. I'm Lee Cone."

Lee was sure this would set Boland off again, but he didn't care. He was about done with Braz

14

Boland, anyhow. Now he was surprised when Jack Dhu beat Boland to it with curt, chill words.

"This is all your fault, Boland, and you know it. Cone told you the herd would break and run if you tried to push it through the pass tonight. You wouldn't listen to him. So, if your pig-headedness is going to cost you money, that's your hard luck. You owe this camp damages. Best pay them."

Lee Cone expected a real explosion from Boland over this. But it did not come, a fact which suggested that Boland didn't have the nerve to face up to Jack Dhu. The best Boland could put up was an evasive grumble.

"I got no money on me now. Won't have until I collect for the horses."

Lee turned to the wagon man, John Vail.

"How much would you figure, friend?"

"The tent cost me thirty dollars and was practically new. Then there was some of the womenfolk's gear in it, which likely ain't much use now. I'll call it square for fifty dollars."

"When I'm paid off for my horses, I'll be back this way," growled Boland, casting an angry glance at Dhu. "Now there's a chore ahead," he announced, "rounding up the herd again. Come on, Dhu, and you . . . Cone."

Boland reined away, with Jack Dhu following him.

Lee Cone lingered for a moment. His glance searched the dark about him, a dark not quite so deep now, for the massing stars were beginning to flood the world with a faint, silver radiance. He could see these people fairly well. There was the older woman with the two still badly frightened youngsters clinging to her skirts. The man, Vail. And, of course, the girl he had saved, the girl with the rich, husky voice, and her pale hair reflecting the star sheen.

John Vail spoke skeptically. "When he's paid off for his horses! That could be a long time from now, far as my claim for damages is concerned. I doubt I'll ever see that fellow again, or his money, either."

Lee Cone built a cigarette, scratched a match across his saddle skirt, cupped it in his hands while he turned it to a full glow, then tipped his head to meet it. The brief bomb of light picked out his features in lean bronze. His words were quiet.

"I'll make a point of it to remind him, Mister Vail. Now I'll say good night to you folks."

He rode away and the night claimed him.

The girl by the wagon stood watching until horse and rider melted into the dark. Then she listened until the sound of hoofs vanished, too.

John Vail spoke more to himself than anyone in his family. "I still doubt I'll ever see any of that damage money. I don't trust saddle hands . . . not any of them."

"John," said his wife, "I don't think that's fair.

16

We're deeply in debt to that young man. Kip, how he got you clear I'll never know."

The girl smiled softly to herself. "But he did, Mother . . . he did."

II

The town of Antelope, as Lee Cone remembered it, had been a small, sleepy place made up of one short street with a run of weathered buildings along either side. Just an average, small cow town, living a lazy, even cadence. It had been two years since he had been there. But how different it was now, he couldn't quite believe.

It was a good four times as big, and from all appearances still growing feverishly. The main street stretched far out and a cross street had been added. New buildings loomed everywhere, garish with raw lumber, and there was more construction under way every way you looked. The clatter of hammers and the whine of saws provided a thin echo to the solid rumble of activity of streets jammed with wagons and people.

It was midafternoon. It had taken that long to round up Braz Boland's horse herd and bring it down the river flats and put it into a newly built corral at the edge of town.

After Boland was satisfied, he had gone to see the man who he said had contracted to buy the horses. He assured the men he'd be back as soon as he closed the deal to pay off those who had helped him bring in the herd.

Now, squatting on their heels against the front of Asa Bingham's old general store, Lee Cone and Jack Dhu waited for Boland to return. Each was sunk deep in his own thoughts.

Lee Cone was recalling the time he had left Maacama Basin and the events that had led to that leaving. That also had been two years ago.

But he hadn't forgotten Lucy Garland. The second she entered his thoughts, he had to remind himself that he had to quit thinking of her as Lucy Garland. He had to remember she had been married and that she was now Mrs. Tasker Scott. But he couldn't help forget what a lot of fine, great dreams had been shot all to hell there!

That dark fateful evening he'd ridden over to Pete Garland's Lazy Dollar headquarters, and found the three of them standing on the ranch house porch. Pete Garland, Lucy Garland, and Tasker Scott. Lucy and Tasker had both been all dressed up. And Pete Garland had given Lee the word bluntly.

" 'Fraid you're a little late for the festivities, Lee. Lucy and Tasker got married this afternoon, 'round one thirty it must've been. Now they got to get ready to head out on their honeymoon."

He finished off by smiling and patting Tasker on the shoulder.

It was as brutal as a blow in the face, unexpected and almost malicious. For Pete, full of big ideas of power and money, had never looked with too much approval on any romantic relationship between Lee and Lucy, for Lee was just a junior partner of Buck Theodore's, and Buck's Flat T Ranch wasn't a big enough prospect for him when it came to his daughter, especially compared to Tasker Scott's prospects.

While Pete Garland spoke, Tasker Scott had listened, grinning, showing a cold, mocking triumph in his pale eyes. If Lucy had shown any sign of remorse or regret, it might have helped. But she just smiled at her dad and Tasker and seemed almost serene in her dark, sultry beauty, serene and uncaring.

The whole affair had left Lee so sick inside that he could think of nothing but a wild desire to get away, as far away as he could.

To that end, he'd almost rode his horse into the ground getting back to the home ranch. There he packed his war bag and then caught up another horse. The last thing he had done was to give Buck Theodore the word.

Good old Buck made no attempt to hold him back. He said he understood, and even wished him luck.

And that night Lee Cone rode out through

Smoky Pass, telling himself that he'd left Maacama Basin behind him forever.

But two years could be a long time, as Lee had found out, and time could do things to a man. It could heal hurts and it could season and toughen him, bring him balance and a sound sense of values and a recognition of obligations, such as he now felt toward Buck Theodore.

Lee's decision to return to Maacama Basin had been as abrupt as the one to leave it. It had come to him as he lay in his blankets one night in the bunkhouse of Boley Jackon's Line Seven headquarters in the Skull Mountain range. One moment he'd been a tired, reasonably content saddle hand, about to doze off in a friendly bunkhouse. The next he was filled with urgency, hardly able to wait until morning so that he could be on his way.

Jack Dhu's soft drawl cut through the preoccupation of Lee Cone's thoughts.

"Here comes pay day, Lee. Wonder who Boland's fancy friend is? Looks like a tinhorn to me."

Lee lifted his head, looked, and went very still. Cutting across the feverish street at a long angle came Braz Boland. With him was a big, floridly handsome man wearing a tall, cream-colored Stetson. The rest of his apparel was in keeping with the hat—a tan silk shirt with a smoothly knotted brown tie, tight whipcord trousers, and expensive, hand-stitched half boots.

Lee spoke softly. "Not that it means anything to you, Jack, but you're looking at Mister Tasker Scott."

Jack Dhu swung his lean head, flashing a quick glance at Lee. "Strong on the *mister,* ain't you?"

"Very."

Boland and his companion dodged ahead of a ramshackle spring wagon, gained the porch of the store, and headed straight for the two saddle hands. Boland swung his arm in their direction, indicating Cone and Dhu.

"Here they are, Mister Scott. Judge for yourself . . . for I don't know enough about either of them to go down the line for them."

Jack Dhu pushed to his feet and, after hesitating only an instant, Lee Cone followed suit.

"Just what in hell is this?" demanded Jack Dhu coldly. "An auction?"

Braz Boland colored angrily under the chill bite of Jack Dhu's words.

"Mister Scott is looking for some saddle hands himself."

"You don't say!" rapped Dhu. "Well, this saddle hand ain't looking for a job. All I'm interested in now is what you owe me. So pay up, Boland! I'm tired of waiting."

Tasker Scott hadn't spoken. He was staring at Lee Cone, all the affability of his expression fading.

Lee showed him a small, tight, mirthless grin, before he addressed the man he had come to despise.

"Surprised, Tasker? Figured you'd seen the last of me? Trails have a way of circling back." Lee paused and looked Scott up and down with a stare that was openly sardonic. "You seem to have prospered, Tasker . . . you surely do. But you shouldn't wear such tight britches . . . shows off your paunch too much. But then, maybe the paunch is the badge of the big operator . . . the successful man."

Tasker Scott had very light blue eyes, which now paled to the color of skim milk, while the floridness of his heavy cheeks deepened to a congested crimson. He turned on Braz Boland angrily.

"Why didn't you tell me this fellow Cone was one of your men?"

Startled, Boland floundered a little.

"I . . . well, hell! How would I know you two had met before? All I know about Cone is that he'd been in Maacama Basin before and could show me the short way across the desert from Carbide Junction. So I hired him on."

Scott put his pale, fuming glance on Lee Cone again. "You'll be smart if you take the same way out, Cone . . . and quick!"

Lee's grin became even more openly mocking.

"I don't know of any reason to rush, Tasker. No

reason at all. In fact, I aim to stick around a while and renew old acquaintances."

The look which came into Tasker Scott's eyes at these words was one of blank, savage hatred—a killing hatred.

This startled Lee. He had never given Tasker Scott cause to hate him that way. They had never been friendly back in the old days, and there had always been a mutual dislike, but as far as Lee was concerned, nothing worse than that. But here, with a few mocking words, he had roused something that was deadly. He stared at Scott, unable to figure it out.

Tasker Scott seemed to gather himself as he returned the stare, as though about to launch himself physically at Lee. Then he turned and plunged away, his boot heels rapping hard and sharp on the worn planks of the store porch.

Jack Dhu looked at Lee with raised eyebrows.

"Man! What you said sure seemed to have twisted the knife in that fellow. I don't think he likes you."

Braz Boland had pulled a wad of currency from a hip pocket. He counted off several bills and handed them to Jack Dhu, who pocketed them and said: "Looks like you made enough off the deal, Boland, to square up with that granger for his tent and other gear that your crazy horses wrecked for him."

Boland grunted, then declared: "To hell with

him! Think I'm sucker enough to let some fool granger gouge me? Let him whistle."

He turned to Lee, stuffing the balance of his money back into his jeans, and squaring himself belligerently.

"The way I figure it, Cone, you owe me money instead of the other way around. I put you up there at point last night to keep the horse herd under control. You didn't do it. You lost your nerve and let them run. I lost four of the best. Two came up with broken legs and had to be shot. Another foundered itself at the river. And the fourth broke its neck falling over the tongue of the wagon at that damned granger camp. When I add up the value of those four broncs, it comes to way over what I might have owed you in wages."

Lee looked at Boland, not sure he was hearing right. Did this fellow actually think he could get away with anything as raw as this? Lee's lips thinned and little knots of muscle bunched at the sides of his jawline.

"If that's your idea of a joke, Boland," he said softly, "consider that I've laughed. Now pay me. Our agreement back in Carbide Junction called for thirty-five dollars, and thirty-five is what I want."

"Joke be damned!" blurted Boland. "Where money is concerned I never joke."

He gave Lee a look from toes to head, then

turned and would have walked off, but Lee caught him by the shoulder and whirled him around.

Lee stood as tall as Boland, though a good fifteen pounds lighter. But Lee was wolf lean about the flanks, with a lot of his weight in the depth of his chest and the breadth of his shoulders. His gray eyes turned dark.

"Thirty-five dollars, Boland," he repeated, his hand digging to Boland's shoulder now. "And while I'm about it . . . fifty more for the granger, John Vail. Long as you don't aim to deliver it to him yourself, I will. So you'd better come across."

Braz Boland jerked his arm free and spread his feet. "Come across, eh? Sure, Cone. Like this!"

He swung savagely at the side of Lee's head.

The manner in which Boland settled his weight on his spread feet had given Lee some inkling of what was coming, and he instinctively dropped his jaw behind a hunched shoulder. That shoulder took up most of the power of Boland's punch, but not all of it. Boland's fist bounced off Lee's shoulders, then skidded across his face, cutting his mouth. Then, before Boland could recover, Lee stepped in and sank his fist into the pit of Boland's stomach.

It was a deadly blow, carrying with it days of accumulating dislike, plus the sharp, cold anger that whipped through Lee when he realized

25

Boland was deliberately intent on beating him out of his hard-earned wages.

Braz Boland, supremely confident that his own surprise blow would end the argument on the spot, was caught with his belly muscles loose and flaccid. The wicked right fist of Lee's, smashing into his solar plexus, brought him far over, gasping and half paralyzed. Lee gave him no chance to recover, but charged in, both fists slashing and clubbing. He straightened Boland up with a looping belt to the mouth and then nailed him full on the point of his sagging jaw.

Boland went off the store porch, rolling into the street's dust, half under the startled hoofs of a buckboard team tethered at the hitch rail.

"All right, Jack," Lee said to Dhu back over his shoulder. "Just so nobody can argue the point later, you collect my wages for me."

"I can do that with pleasure!" chortled Jack Dhu. "Your wages, and the granger's damages. I'll do it, even though I hate to touch this cheating *hombre*. Why, the damned, crooked whelp . . . trying to pull a blazer like that!"

Braz Boland was so nearly out, he showed no move of resistance as Jack Dhu bent over him, pulled out the wad of currency, counted out eighty-five dollars, then shoved the rest back into Boland's pocket.

Straightening up, Jack Dhu grinned wickedly.

"No, he shouldn't have tried that. When he gets through gagging for air, he'll realize that himself. I never saw anybody get hit harder. Cone, you surprise me. I never figured you were that tough."

Lee said nothing as he pocketed the money. Then he jerked his head. "Let's get out of here before a crowd gathers and begins asking questions."

"Get out where?"

"I know a ranch we can bunk at for a few days while we figure out what our future plans are."

Jack Dhu shook his head. "I got no future plans. Gave up that foolishness a long time ago. Planning the future always makes life complicated. Besides, coming across that damned desert left me with a long thirst. But I'll probably be seeing you around."

Lee didn't argue. He'd come to like Jack Dhu, but he'd also recognized a certain wild streak in the man, and a deadly one, if aroused.

"All right, Jack," he said. "That's a promise. I'll be seeing you around."

Lee had left his horse tied at the far end of the store's hitch rail. Now he freed the reins, stepped into the saddle, and threaded a way through the crush of wagons on the street. There was a warm moistness seeping down his chin and when he scrubbed a hand across the spot it came away stained crimson. He dabbed at his cut lips with the tail of his neckerchief, while another twist of anger went through him. That sure had been a raw one Boland had tried to pull.

Nearing the edge of town, the jam on the street forced Lee to rein in while a big freight outfit, lead wagon, and back action, creaked ponderously by. Just behind the freighter came an open-topped buggy, bright and new and sparkling in the sun. A matched team of spirited bay horses drew the rig, and handling the reins with deft control was the person Lee Cone had been trying for two years to forget.

She saw Lee the moment he saw her and with that recognition she pulled back on the reins and drew her fretting team to a halt. Her dark eyes widened and her full lips parted breathlessly.

"Lee!" she cried. "Lee Cone!"

Lee touched his hat. "Hello, Lucy. Or maybe that's being too familiar. . . . Maybe I'd better change that. Missus Scott, how are you?" Lee couldn't keep a touch of bitter irony from his tone.

She was just as beautiful as she'd been back in the days when she had so completely blinded his eyes and his heart—her dark eyes, her raven-black hair, her willful, crimson mouth.

He saw her flinch slightly at his words, but her glance did not waver.

"I'll forgive you that, Lee, for perhaps I deserve

28

it. But now . . . Oh, it's good to see you again! I want to talk to you."

Lee stared at her soberly, then shook his head. "I'm afraid your husband would object to that, Missus Scott. Our chance to talk came a long time ago. We did a lot of it back then, concerning our relationship and what we could do with the future. But apparently it didn't mean a thing. And now . . . considering where we both ended up . . . I can't think of any kind of talk that could do either of us any good."

He touched his hat again, gigged his horse and rode on.

III

Tasker Scott's office took up a corner of the first floor of a big, two-story, newly built warehouse. He was pacing back and forth, chewing on an unlighted cigar, when the door opened and his wife came in. He turned on her angrily.

"What are you doing in town?"

She looked him up and down coolly. "Because I felt like riding in," she replied tartly. "That was part of the bargain . . . remember? You do as you please, and I do as I please." She studied him again for a moment, then added: "I see that you know about it, too."

"Know about what?"

"Lee Cone is back."

He flared at her. "You've seen him . . . talked to him?"

She shrugged her shapely shoulders. "I saw him. I'd like to have a talk with him, but he didn't seem very interested. Not that I blame him, of course."

"You'll leave him alone. You'll stay away from him, understand!"

Lucy Scott looked her husband up and down again. "You always were a jealous fool, Tasker. Jealous of all your possessions. Greedy, too."

He barked a harsh, mirthless laugh. "You should talk about greed!"

She nodded and spoke evenly. "You're quite right there, Tasker. We're very greedy people, you and I. Two of a kind. A fact I realized when I married you. Probably the main reason I did marry you. I saw in you a man who could get me the things I wanted in life."

"Just the material things?" he said.

It was her turn to laugh without mirth. "You never knew about the more tender emotions, Tasker. Let's not turn sentimental . . . it would be a very poor act. Now let's come down to cases. What are we going to do about him?"

"What do you mean?"

"You know exactly what I mean. Lee Cone is back. What about him?"

Tasker Scott dropped into the chair behind

his desk. He tried to light his cigar, found it too badly frayed, threw it aside, pulled a fresh one from his breast pocket, and lit this. He scowled into the smoke for a moment before he answered.

"I'll take care of Lee Cone. I ran him out of Maacama Basin before. I'll do it again."

"That's a very empty boast," said Lucy Scott smoothly. "You ran nobody out of Maacama Basin. Let's consider a few facts. Lee Cone left Maacama Basin because he was hurt emotionally. He's had time to get over that. Now he's back. He'll be looking up Buck Theodore and he'll hear about the ranch. I doubt very much that he'll take that lying down. He could cause us a great deal of trouble."

Tasker Scott shook his head, blew out a mouthful of smoke. "Not that way," he assured her. "There isn't a thing he could do to hurt me that way. He can't prove a thing."

"I hope not. You've traveled pretty fast, Tasker . . . maybe too fast to cover your back trail."

He pounded a fist on the desk. "I don't like that kind of talk, especially from you. Makes me out a crook."

She laughed again. "You wouldn't try to make me believe you're a thoroughly honest man, would you?"

Tasker Scott grew quiet as he studied her with narrowed eyes. "You are the most beautiful woman I ever saw," he said, "and the most cold-

31

blooded. There have been others like you in history, and every now and then a man has come along who knew just how to handle them. It's high time you were handled the same way."

He was out of his chair and had her by the arm before she could move. His fingers pinched deep and she twisted at the pain and tried to pull loose.

"Let go of me!" she cried.

Instead, he jerked her close and kissed her hungrily. He held her away from him and jeered at her. "My loving wife! From now on, when I bark, you bounce!"

She pulled back her free hand and slapped him across the face. Instantly he was shaking her, shaking her until her head snapped loosely and her hair fell across her shoulders.

There was that burning in his eyes that was worse than the physical manhandling.

When he let go of her, she leaned weakly against the wall. And for the first time, Lucy Scott was physically afraid of her husband.

Tasker Scott saw that fear in her eyes, and laughed.

"Now," he said, "we actually understand each other. I see that I should have brought this understanding about earlier. A final word to you, my dear. Stay away from Lee Cone."

She did not answer. With unsteady fingers she tidied up her hair and smoothed her dress. Then she went out, passing Braz Boland just beyond the door.

Boland stared at her curiously, then went on in. Boland's lips were puffed, one side of his jaw was lumpy. His breathing was a little unsteady.

Tasker Scott faced him harshly. "What in hell do you want?"

"Where will I find the law in this town?"

"There isn't any yet. What do you have in mind?"

Boland told him, concluding with: "He went off with eighty-five dollars of my money, Cone did. I was down and couldn't do anything about it. But I heard what was said. That was robbery, Mister Scott. And I want something done about it."

Scott considered him narrowly for a moment, then nodded.

"Pull up a chair, Boland. I think we can do business." Scott shuffled around in one of his desk drawers before leaning back and saying: "No, there isn't any law in this town right now, so maybe we'd better set up some. How would you like to be town marshal?"

Boland stared, before he exploded: "Me! Town marshal?"

"Why not? Cone will continue to stay in town for a while, probably. Be a lot of satisfaction in slapping an arrest on him yourself, wouldn't it? And," added Scott smoothly, "maybe he'd try and resist. In which case . . ." Scott ended with a shrug.

Their glances met, and both men smiled.

"You got a badge?" asked Boland.

"I got a badge," answered Scott, and produced one from a desk drawer.

IV

The ranch headquarters lay on the southern point of a little flat tucked back into the tawny flank of the Mineral Hills. Riding up to the layout and marking its well-remembered outlines, eagerness deepened and shone in Lee Cone's eyes. It was good to be back.

Yet, in a moment, some of that first enthusiasm left him. For the place had taken on a run-down beaten look. There were only two horses in the cavvy corral. A thin spire of pale smoke seeped from the chimney of the main cabin and Lee reined over that way.

A man stepped from the door of the place, a stringy-looking jasper with a straggly mustache and eyes as hard and unrevealing as a pair of glass beads. A belt gun sagged at one lank thigh and across his arm lay a Winchester carbine.

The fellow looked Lee over with deliberateness, spat, then spoke with a nasal drawl.

"Looking for somebody?"

"Yeah," answered Lee. "I am. For Buck Theodore."

The man with the carbine spat again. "Never heard of him."

A stir of mingled anger and alarm ran through Lee. But caution whispered in his ear. Something was wrong here. It would pay to play it cagy.

"Two years ago," said Lee, "a man named Buck Theodore lived here. I've been away. Thought I'd drop by and say hello."

The man with the carbine turned his head and called over his shoulder. "Hey, Stump . . . you ever hear of a Buck Theodore?"

A second man crowded out the door. He was broad and squat, with a tangle of red hair above a round, pock-marked face. He also had a gun at his hip.

"What'cha want with Theodore?" he demanded.

"Knew him some time back," said Lee. "Just thought I'd look him up while I was passing through."

He underwent another close scrutiny by the pair of them. Lee looked as guileless and casual as he could.

Finally Stump spoke. "There's an old coot holding down a cabin over on Laurel Creek. Heard his name was Theodore. That's the creek, ain't it, Pecos . . . the third one over to the west?"

The other nodded. "That's right . . . Laurel Creek."

Lee Cone nodded. "Obliged. I know the creek you mean. I'll take a ride out there now."

He reined away, back the way he had come, and it wasn't until he was well beyond rifle shot of the place that the tension ran out of him. He kept thinking that that carbine held by the fellow called Pecos by Stump might be leveled at his back. He'd just left a pair of hardcases, that was for sure.

He couldn't understand why Buck Theodore wasn't at the old headquarters, but it was a relief to know that Buck was alive. He knew the cabin on Laurel Creek. It was a line camp cabin, shared equally in the old days by the Flat T and Pete Garland's Lazy Dollar.

Lee set his horse straight for it and rode in there just at sunset.

At first glance the place looked deserted. Then Lee saw the horse in the pole corral out back. He sent a low call.

"Buck! Hey, Buck!"

He got his second shock of the day at sight of the man who stepped from the doorway. It was Buck Theodore all right, but a different man than Lee remembered. His hair was almost white, and he had gaunt, stooped shoulders and a seamed, weary face.

"Buck! It's Lee . . . Lee Cone!" he called out almost hesitantly.

Buck Theodore straightened and stared, blinking,

as though scarcely crediting his own eyes. When words came the voice was deep and hollow and somehow empty.

"Lee! I'll be damned. . . ."

Lee's laugh was shaky as he dropped from his saddle to grip the old fellow's hand.

"Buck! It's great to see you again."

"You ain't seeing much, boy. Just a busted flush that'll never rate another deal. Kid, where you been? Where you been?"

There was something almost like a plaintive cry in these last words, a cry that cut deep into Lee.

"Just drifting, Buck. I been away too long."

The old fellow made an effort to straighten his shoulders. "Mebbe it wouldn't have made any difference if you'd been here. Most likely Tasker Scott would have been too strong for both of us. Anyway, it's gone . . . our ranch is gone. Scott's got it. He took it away from me. I let you down, boy."

Now Lee began to understand. "You didn't let me down, Buck. I let you down. I ran like a whipped pup, when I should have stayed."

Old Buck dropped a hand on Lee's shoulder. "Ain't blaming you, boy, ain't blaming you a bit. In your shoes I'd have done the same . . . mebbe worse. No, it's not your fault. I know all the fine plans you'd made. I remember how you used to talk them over with me. And then Lucy Garland left you flat and married Tasker Scott. A deal like that was enough to toss any man. And while it's no comfort to you it's pretty common knowledge that by this time Lucy realizes she made a damned poor choice."

"I wonder," muttered Lee. "Not that she knows, but that she cares."

"Wouldn't know," said Buck. "Some women's minds can run strange. But Pete Garland sure got what he asked for. Pete died last spring. I heard he died of shame, because his prize son-in-law plumb finagled him out of everything he had, including his shirt. But shuck that saddle, boy, and turn your bronc' into the corral. I was just fixing to have some supper. Sure good to have you here again. Makes me feel it's worthwhile to go on living."

Buck turned back into the cabin, blowing his nose loudly.

In the gravest frame of mind he'd known in a long time, Lee Cone unsaddled and turned his horse into the corral. A blinding sense of guilt held him. He'd expected nothing like this in Maacama Basin. The ranch gone. Good old Buck reduced to living like an old pack rat in a tumbledown line cabin. And all because he himself had let a sultry, black-haired, dark-eyed girl make a fool of him.

When Lee went into the cabin, Buck Theodore had a fire going in the old stove and was banging pots and pans around. The old cabin was as clean and neat as it was possible to make it.

"About the ranch, Buck? Tell me how it happened," Lee asked.

Buck stoked the fire again before answering. "Like I said, it was Tasker Scott. Slick *hombre*, that fellow, slick as grease. He rustled me blind. He kept hiring riders away from me. No matter what I'd pay a saddle hand, Scott would pay him more. So I had to try and hold things together on my own. I tried, all right. I worked twenty hours a day but I couldn't be everywhere at once. I'd miss a few cattle here and there and while I was trying to trail 'em down, another bunch would disappear somewhere else." Buck paused and shrugged. "A year and a half of that kind of working over and I was all done."

"And the ranch?" Lee asked.

Buck shrugged again. "Had to borrow money to keep going. Asa Bingham let me have three thousand dollars on a twelve-month note, with the spread as collateral. Not six months later, Scott showed up with that note, wanting the money. He'd bought the note from Bingham. I couldn't rake up the money, which Scott well knew. Oh, I could have stalled him off, I reckon, until the due date. But I wouldn't have had the money then, either. I was tired of fighting something I couldn't stop. So I just got the hell out from under the whole damned mess. Had I been ten years younger, I'd have throwed a gun on Tasker Scott and shot his heart out."

"The cattle he rustled . . . where did they end up?" asked Lee.

"God knows. I sure don't. I've prowled this basin from end to end and I ain't seen a single beef critter packing our old Flat T brand. Scott must have drove 'em out to the railroad. All water under the bridge now, boy."

"Maybe," said Lee softly. "Maybe."

"You come in through Antelope, boy?"

"Yeah, I came through town."

"Then," said Buck, "you saw how things is changed. We got a land rush on in Maacama Basin. I've heard it said that Tasker Scott engineered that, so he could clean up on all the property he bought up ahead of it. He just about owns everything in Antelope and roundabout. He's even made his gamble on cashing in when the railroad comes to Maacama Basin."

"How's that?" Lee demanded.

Buck scooped flour into a pan, began mixing up some biscuit dough.

"There always has been talk that someday the railroad would build into Maacama Basin. Now with the country filling up with grangers, it's more likely than ever. Only two ways a railroad could come in. Either by the river gap, or by Smoky Pass. And who do you think has got the property sewed up in both places? Why, Tasker

Scott, of course. He bought out old Manuel Rojas down in the river gap before the land rush started, and got the property dirt cheap. And he holds most the land this side of Smoky Pass, where the railroad would have to cut through. I'm telling you, boy, that fellow Scott don't miss a trick."

"How did he get hold of the land at Smoky Pass?" asked Lee. "That was government land, open for homesteading, yes, but not for sale."

"I dunno how he got it, but he's got it," said Buck. "I checked up in the Land Office and all that slope this side of the pass is blocked in solid . . . under Tasker Scott's name."

"But he couldn't do that, Buck," argued Lee. "He couldn't take that land without going through all the homesteading rules, occupancy and improvements . . . all that sort of thing."

"Boy," said Buck gently, "in Maacama Basin, Tasker Scott does just about as he pleases. When he cracks the whip, even them in the Land Office dance. He's as crooked as a broken-backed snake, but he's the slickest article ever to hit these parts."

Lee got out the makings and rolled a cigarette. He paced the short area of the cabin, sunk in thought. Half to himself, he murmured: "There never was a crook who didn't overlook some angle. And I got one angle in mind I'm sure going to take a long look at."

Buck Theodore came around to face him.

41

"Lee, you've come back to something mighty tough to swallow. But the best thing you can do is swallow and forget, because you can't buck this fellow Scott. He's got money, power, and guns behind him. Don't you go getting any foolish ideas. You're still young and got lots of time. You can make a new start somewhere else. There ain't sense in running a chance of getting yourself killed for nothing."

Lee showed a thin, tight smile. "I ran, Buck. But no more. I learned a few things while I was on the drift. Maybe I learned a trick or two Tasker Scott isn't up to. Did you ever give Scott a bill of sale for anything?"

Buck stared. "Hell no! What's that got to do with it?"

Lee's grin widened. "Why that, Buck, is the angle Tasker overlooked. And it can hang him!"

V

Early morning sunup showed the town of Antelope only slightly less active than it had been the previous afternoon. Leaving his horse in front of Bingham's store, Lee Cone headed for the Land Office. Three doors along, where a saloon front ran, Lee paused beside a lank figure hunkered down where the first sunlight struck.

"Get rid of that thirst, Jack?" Lee asked.

Jack Dhu's head came up slowly and he stared at Lee for a moment out of bloodshot eyes. Then he grinned crookedly.

"Swapped it for a hell of a headache."

"Reckless man," commented Lee. "Had breakfast?"

Jack Dhu considered this for a moment, feeling cautiously of his pockets. Then he said: "Ain't hungry."

"A cheerful liar," observed Lee. "Come along. I'm buying. And don't go stiff necked on me."

Jack Dhu pushed to his feet. "Have a good look at a damned fool," he said wryly. "I'm taking you up on your offer because right now I need black coffee like a drowning man needs air."

They turned into an eating house a little farther along.

Lee said: "We'll eat first and talk later. I got a proposition that might interest you, Jack."

When they emerged, half an hour later, Jack Dhu built a cigarette and said: "I'm beginning to live again. Short of walking on my hands, I'll trail along on anything you want to do, Lee."

"Then," Lee responded, "let's go over to the Land Office."

The Land Office had just opened for business. Inside, Lee called for a map of the west end of the basin. He studied this for a time, then turned to the clerk.

"These blocked in areas show land already taken up?"

The clerk nodded. "That's right."

"And the map's up to date?"

"To the minute. We got to keep them that way, or we'd have title arguments all over the place."

Lee traced a forefinger over a certain area. "Who homesteaded these quarter sections?"

The clerk was sharp-featured and fancied himself as a dandy. When he glanced at the area Lee indicated, his manner underwent a subtle change. Officious haughtiness began to show.

"What's it matter who homesteaded them?" he finally answered. "The map shows the land is taken up."

Lee spread both hands on the counter, fixed the clerk with a chill glance. "Friend, I asked you a straight question. I expect a straight answer."

"That's right," put in Jack Dhu as he moved closer to the counter. "We ain't a couple of scared grangers who can be buffaloed by a ten-cent squirt like you. Talk up, and you'd better talk straight."

The clerk's haughty look became a harried one. These cowboys had a tough look to them, too tough for him to fool with.

"I'll check," he said hastily. "Take a couple of minutes."

He turned and dug into a file case, came up with a couple of papers.

"These records show the land was taken up by Mister Scott . . . Mister Tasker Scott."

Lee Cone grinned. "Knew that all the time, didn't you? Now tell me . . . did Tasker Scott actually homestead that land strictly according to law? Did he fulfill the occupancy and improvement conditions?"

The clerk drifted from a harried condition to a confused and flustered one. "Why, I suppose. I mean I guess he did. You'd have to see Mister Wilkens about that. Mister Wilkens is the land agent. I only work here."

Lee's grin widened. "Thanks, friend. But from now on you better stick to the truth. Because you're a damned poor liar."

When they went out, Lee said: "Get your horse, Jack. I'll wait for you in front of Bingham's store."

Jack Dhu nodded and angled off, and Lee went along to the store.

Asa Bingham was sweeping out the place when Lee walked in. He paused, a gaunt figure, rested on his broom, and fixed Lee with a not too friendly eye.

Lee said: "Hi, Asa. Long time no see."

The storekeeper grunted. "High time you were showing back in Maacama Basin, Cone. You sure left Buck Theodore to take a hell of a beating."

Lee met Bingham's accusing glance steadily. "I did, didn't I. But how about that note you sold to Tasker Scott? That didn't help Buck any."

The storekeeper flushed. "Biggest mistake I ever made in my life. I didn't know Scott then like I know him now. He gave me his solemn word he wouldn't press Buck. I was short of cash at the time, which is why I sold. I've felt like hell about it ever since it happened."

Lee slapped the storekeeper on the shoulder. "Forget it, Asa. We all make mistakes. Buck will probably come out all right, after all."

Bingham's manner thawed a little as he leaned the broom by the door. "You back in Maacama Basin to stay?" he asked Lee.

"I've been thinking about," Lee answered.

"Aiming to do anything special?"

"Yeah. I'm going to have one hell of a try at getting the ranch back."

Bingham pinched his bony chin with thumb and forefinger. "Tough chore. Tasker Scott's got this basin by the throat. But I sure wish you luck."

While Lee and the storekeeper were talking, a man had been working his way down the street. It was Braz Boland. He came up on the far end of the store porch, and was well along it when Lee, hearing the steps, turned.

He found himself looking into the muzzle of Boland's gun. Lee stiffened, rocked up on his toes.

"Easy does it, Cone!" growled Boland. "Don't try and go for your gun. You're under arrest!"

Lee went still, staring at the badge on Boland's shirt front. "Under arrest! What for?"

"You know damned well what for. Robbery. Get your hands up!"

Lee lifted his hands slowly until they were level with his ears. "Just who did I rob? And when did this happen exactly?"

"Yesterday. You robbed me . . . you and that fellow Dhu. You went through my pockets and took my money."

"Not your money, Boland," stated Lee. "Mine! The wages you owed me and tried to get out of paying. Yeah, my wages and what you owed John Vail for damages. That wasn't robbery, Boland."

"It was robbery!" snapped Boland. "And you don't get away with a thing like that here in Antelope. I'm taking you in."

Lee spoke to Asa Bingham without turning his head. "Who appoints the town marshal, Asa?"

"First I knew that this town had one," answered the storekeeper. "But since you asked me, I'd say this smells of some more of Tasker Scott's high and mighty ways to me. And if Scott put this jigger in as marshal, then he's sure to be a crook."

"I think so, too, Asa," Lee said softly. "Boland, you can't get away with arresting me."

"Can't I, though?" jeered Boland. "Let's see you stop me. I'm taking your gun, Cone . . . and I just hope you try and keep me from it. I hope you

47

lower your hands just one short inch. Then I'll fix you . . . and plenty! The way you deserve to be fixed."

Boland came edging in, his gun bearing steadily on Lee's body.

Lee read the look in Boland's eyes, and knew that on the merest thread of an excuse, Boland would smoke him down.

Through the alley at the far end of the store, Jack Dhu came riding. As he turned into the street, he took in the threatening tableau on the store porch. Instantly a gun was in his hand and his words hit out in bleak harshness.

"Drop that gun, Boland! You ain't got long. Drop it!"

Braz Boland grunted as though struck by a blow. His head jerked around.

Jack Dhu came riding along, just outside the hitch rail, and the gun he held was all cold menace.

Boland dropped his gun and backed up a step or two.

"Smart," said Jack Dhu. "Now, what's this all about?"

Lee, lowering his arms, explained.

Dhu showed a hard grin. "No way! This big-mouthed four-flusher a marshal? That's an insult to decent men. Take off that badge, Boland! Take it off and throw it in the street!"

Boland's bluster was weak as dishwater. "I was

hired to wear this badge. I got authority. . . ."

"You got no more authority than a sheep-killing coyote," cut in Jack Dhu coldly. "You heard me, Boland, take that badge off and throw it in the street, or I'll shoot it off you."

Braz Boland licked his lips, fumbled at the badge, tossed it out into the street's dust.

"Now get out of here," Dhu ordered contemptuously. "This is the second blazer you've tried to run. If you try a third one, I'll make it my personal chore to run you down and pistol whip you to rags. Get out of here, now."

Boland turned and hurried away down the street.

VI

At the edge of the river below the John Vail camp, it was wash day. There was a brisk fire, with buckets of water heating above it. There was a galvanized washtub set on a flat rock where Kip Vail was up to her elbows in sudsy foam, scrubbing industriously on a washboard. One line of wash, strung between two trees, was already drying.

The girl was humming to herself as she worked, and even at this homely chore, every move was one of slim, strong grace. The terror of the night of the horse stampede was something already

49

forgotten, for such is the way of youth. But other circumstances of that night, Kip Vail told herself, she'd never forget—like the steely strength of the arm that had caught her up and carried her to safety, the sound of that man's voice, and the hard, clean bronze of his face as picked out by match light when he lit a cigarette. Kip smiled to herself and tried to blow aside a lock of hair that had fallen down across her face.

The click of hoofs on a gravel bar made her straighten up and turn. To her surprise, she found herself looking up at the very man she'd been thinking about. That stubborn lock of hair had fallen down across her face again and when, forgetful of the suds on her hands, she tried to brush it hastily aside, she left a soapy smear across one smooth, brown cheek.

Lee Cone chuckled. "Reminds me of a little tune or jingle my mother used to say. 'There was a little girl, and she had a little curl, right in the middle of her forehead. . . .' "

"And when she was good, she was very, very good, and when she was bad she was horrid," cut in Kip.

Lee shook his head. "I doubt that last part. It doesn't fit."

"That," said Kip, "is because you don't know me very well. You should see me when I'm really stirred up. Dad says I should have red hair to match my temper."

Startled at first, she was now completely at ease.

Lee Cone, looking at her, thought that this girl would always be poised and self-reliant. He thought other things, too. Her eyes were a clear blue, and entirely honest. For no good reason, he found himself comparing her with Lucy Garland, and he was startled by the realization that she in no way suffered by contrast.

She did not have Lucy's full, sultry beauty, but she had a clearness and a freshness about her. She colored a little under the unconscious intentness of his glance.

"If I look a fright," she said, smiling, "it's because it's that kind of a day. Whoever looked their best up to their eyes in soapsuds?"

"I was just thinking," said Lee, "that you most likely look your best under any conditions."

Now her cheeks flamed and her eyes dropped.

Lee, with discernment, changed the subject. "Where's your father?"

John Vail answered that himself by coming up with another armful of wood for the fire. He nodded to Lee, but with no great friendliness. John Vail had the common feeling of grangers toward men of the saddle. He was distrustful of them, and, moreover, he didn't like the warm color in his daughter's cheeks and the shine in her eyes, just because this particular man of the saddle was talking to her.

Lee stepped from his saddle, reached into the

pocket of his shirt, and drew out some folded greenbacks.

"Came by to take care of that damage claim of yours, Mister Vail. You said fifty dollars would cover it . . . so here's your money."

John Vail stared at the money laid in his palm, then spoke gruffly. "This surprises me. I never expected to collect. That fellow Boland didn't act too happy over the idea of paying. He struck me as being on the slippery side . . . meaning no offense, if he's a friend of yours."

"No friend of mine," assured Lee. "And he . . . decided to pay."

John Vail, no fool, looked at Lee shrewdly. "What made him decide?"

Lee met Vail's glance and grinned. "This and that."

Vail pocketed the money and put out his hand, his manner mellowing. "Let's shake. It's a pleasure to meet a square saddle man. Looks like we're in your debt, after what you did for Kip here, and then this."

"Lots of square saddle men out there, Mister Vail," said Lee briefly, as they shook hands. "Just a question of meeting up with them."

He paused to build a cigarette, then turned back to his horse. "Got to be getting along. Long way to Carbide Junction."

Kip Vail, listening and watching, gave a soft little exclamation of dismay.

John Vail said: "Carbide Junction? You mean you're pulling out of Maacama Basin?"

"Just for a few days," Lee told him. "Got some business to look into over that way. I'll drop in on my way back, if it's all right with you."

"You do that," Vail said heartily. "Stop in and have a meal with us."

Lee stepped into his saddle, and sent his horse splashing across the river shallows.

On the far bank he turned in his saddle and looked back. Kip Vail was watching him. He lifted an arm in salute and she waved back. It seemed he could feel the warmth of her smile, even at this distance.

Carbide Junction's main claim to existence was that of a water stop on the railroad, that and a spread of cattle shipping pens. There was a combined hotel and eating establishment of sorts, a store, two saloons, a station house, and a dozen odd shanties.

The station agent's name was Turner. He was short, stout, genial, and just lazy enough to be contented with a minor job entailing little responsibility and less real work. He was brewing a pot of coffee on the station house stove when Lee Cone came in, dragging his spurs.

The dust of hard travel lay thick on Lee, and he was worn and sunken-eyed with weariness. He sniffed the fragrance of the coffee avidly, but got right down to business.

"Want you to do me a favor, friend," he said, nodding toward the telegraph key on the table in a far corner of the room. "Take hold of that and drop a call to Jeff Barron at Crestline. Reckon you've wire talked with Jeff many a time?"

Turner looked Lee over, then nodded. "It'll cost you money if it's a business message."

"Not exactly business," explained Lee. "Though I can stand a couple of dollars if that's the way it has to be." He paused and eyed Turner. "Mainly, I just wanted you to ask Jeff if he knows a guy named Lee Cone, and if Cone is a friend of his. The whole thing adds up by way of being an introduction. You see, I'm Lee Cone."

"Which," said Turner shrewdly, "adds up that you may be asking another favor of me. Right?"

"That's right."

Turner went over to the key, threw a switch, and then rattled out a series of station calls.

Almost immediately the answer came clacking back. Turner sent and received messages for a couple of minutes, his eyes beginning to twinkle and a smile splitting his round face.

Presently he signed off and turned around to face Lee.

"Jeff Barron said this fellow Cone is a damned highbinder at the game, two-handed pedro," the agent smiled, waiting for a reaction from Cone,

54

but Cone remained static. Turner continued: "But he also said he'd do to ride the river with, and that if he wanted to borrow ten dollars to let him have it, and that he'd guarantee the loan."

Lee grinned wearily and shook his head. "Not money I want. But I could stand a cup of that coffee, and later on that second favor."

Turner swung open the wicket in the counter. "Come on in." Then, noting the eagerness with which Lee reached for a cup of coffee, he added: "How would a plate of ham and potatoes go with that coffee?"

"Man," exclaimed Lee, "you make me rubber-legged with the thought!"

Half an hour later, fed and relaxed, Lee spoke through a cloud of cigarette smoke.

"Maybe I'm going to ask you to break a regulation, Mister Turner. But I'd like the chance to look over some of your past cattle shipping records. Don't know how far back they go and how long you keep them, but the longer you hold onto them the better."

"I have them a couple of years back, at least," Turner responded. "Two or three times I been of a mind to burn some of the older ones, but there's always a chance that some smart young beaver of an auditor will come through and want to dig into ancient stuff just out of damned orneriness. About regulations . . . well, it's fun to bust 'em once in a while. How far back you want to start?"

"A year or year and a half should be about right," Cone told him.

From a shelf under the counter, Turner produced several twine wrapped bundles of shipping invoices. He glanced at some dates, then handed one of the bundles to Lee.

"Try this one."

Lee began poring through the bundle. Presently he gave a low exclamation of satisfaction.

Turner threw him a sharp glance. "Find something interesting?"

"Plenty!" exulted Lee. "Listen to this," he said, then read:

> One hundred and thirty head of Hereford cattle. Primary brand, Flat T. Vented to Lazy Dollar. Consigned to Gimball & Reese, Kansas City. Shipped by T.R. Scott.

"Sounds regular enough," observed Turner. "What's so interesting about it?"

"To my knowledge," said Lee, "T.R. Scott neglected to pay for . . . or get a bill of sale . . . for any Flat T cattle that he vented to Lazy Dollar."

"Ouch!" exclaimed Turner. "That could be bad."

"Very bad," Lee said, then grinned. "At least for T.R. Scott."

He laid the invoice aside and looked for others. He found one that listed a straight shipment of Flat T cattle, vented to Lazy Dollar, to add to the first. He found two others showing a mixed shipment of Lazy Dollar with some Flat T, vented. All consigned to the same destination, all shipped by T.R. Scott.

He leaned back. "These are enough. If I can't put the dead wood on that jigger with these, then I couldn't with a hundred. You got some place you can put these particular ones, Mister Turner, where nobody can lay hands on them but yourself?"

Turner nodded toward an iron safe against the far wall. "That should do the job for us."

Lee built another cigarette before saying gravely: "I hope this won't cause you any trouble. You know there's a chance that Scott will get wind of this and try to get hold of the invoices. If he does, he'll be in a bad frame of mind."

"Know what you mean," said Turner.

His round, amiable face suddenly seemed leaner and harder. He reached under the counter again and came up with a sawed-off shotgun. "A couple of times in the past I've had occasion to flash this. I can do it again. Packs a lot of authority. Those invoices will be here right where I put them, should you ever want them again."

Lee stood up, stretched. "You've been mighty

fine. Don't know what I can do by way of thanks."

Turner waved a dismissing hand. "Any friend of Jeff Barron's is a friend of mine. This fellow Scott hangs out in Maacama Basin, doesn't he?"

Lee nodded. "That's right. Going to be my stamping ground from now on, too."

"Then I'll probably see you again," said Turner. "There's some pretty straight talk drifting through the channels that because of this land rush into Maacama Basin, the railroad is going to build a branch line from here across the desert and into Maacama Basin by way of Smoky Pass. When that happens, I'm going to put in for the station agent job there."

"When you show up," promised Lee, "we'll sure kill the fatted calf. Now, I got to be traveling again. Once more . . . thanks!"

Lee led his weary horse down to the general store, stocked up on a little food, filled his canteen with water, and sacked a couple of good feeds of oats for his mount. Then he headed back into the desert.

John Vail was breaking camp. With Kip and her mother helping, he was loading all his gear into the big wagon. Most of the job was finished when Lee Cone came riding down the slope from Smoky Pass, dusty, unshaven, saddle worn.

At sight of Lee, Kip Vail's eyes shone for a

moment, before going grave and troubled once more.

Lee touched his hat to her and her mother.

"Looks like you folks are packing up. What's the matter?"

John Vail answered, wearily gruff: "We're pulling out. With a family like I got, I can't afford any trouble."

"Trouble! What kind of trouble?"

"They claimed I'm on land already filed on," growled Vail. Then, with a sudden show of anger: "They must be lying. Look around, Cone. Do you see any signs of occupancy besides me and mine? Do you see any signs of improvements being made? They were lying. But there's trouble ahead if I stay, and I'm in no position to fight."

Lee slouched sideways in his saddle, built a cigarette. "Tell me about it," he urged quietly.

"There were two of them," explained Vail. "Hardcases, both. They showed up right after breakfast this morning. They told me I was on land already taken up, and that I had to get off. When I demanded proof, one of them put a hand on his gun and said that was all the proof necessary. They said they'd be back tomorrow morning, and if I hadn't moved they'd move me off. So . . ." Vail shrugged.

"These two," asked Lee, "what did they look like?"

"One was heavy-set, pock-marked, and with red hair. The other . . ."

"Lank and stringy-looking, with a ragged mustache," Lee supplied.

Vail's head came up. "How did you know?"

"I've met those two buckos," Lee said succinctly. "Go by the names of Stump and Pecos. Tasker Scott's men."

"Tasker Scott! I can't hardly believe that!" exclaimed Vail. "I understood that Tasker Scott was very friendly toward grangers. In fact, he's the man who encouraged us to come to Maacama Basin."

"Probably did"—Lee nodded—"for his own profit. Mister Vail, you know your own business. But before you give up your claim, think on this. You've filed on what could be one of the most valuable pieces of ground in the whole basin. There's strong talk that the railroad is going to build a spur line out from Carbide Junction that will come into Maacama Basin by way of Smoky Pass, up yonder." Lee pointed toward the pass. "If it does . . . and I think it's going to . . . they'll be wanting right of way across some of your claim, and they'll pay good money for it. That's why Tasker Scott wants you off this land, so he can claim it and be the one to collect on the railroad deal when it comes through."

John Vail squared himself. "You giving it to me

straight, Cone? The railroad is really coming in?"

"All I can tell you is that it's been rumored for a long time that when and if Maacama Basin was really settled up, the railroad would come in. I've just returned from Carbide Junction. While I was there I had a talk with the station agent. He told me the talk all along the line was that the railroad was going to build that spur . . . through Smoky Pass."

John Vail stared up toward the pass and let his glance rove across the slope, as though visualizing how the railroad grade would run.

"You're right," he finally stated. "That line would have to cross part of my land. If I didn't have a family, I'd give those fellows the fight of their lives. I'd . . ."

Mrs. Vail walked up beside her husband and placed her hand on his shoulder.

"You will, anyhow, John Vail," she said. "We have every right in the world to this land. We filed on it according to law and regulation. We've occupied it and are ready to start with the improvements. It means a home and security for us. We're not going to let a couple of bullies with guns run us out."

"Mother's right, Dad," put in Kip.

Lee Cone flashed an admiring glance at the two women before addressing John Vail. "With that kind of backing, you can't lose. And just so you'll feel better about it, you won't be putting up a fight by yourself. You'll have friends to back your hand."

"What friends? Mighty few people we know in this basin, and them only casually."

"You can count on me and two others, for sure," said Lee. "And if that isn't enough, then we'll tell the other settlers what Tasker Scott is trying to do to you . . . and why. The effect of that will give Scott plenty to worry about."

John Vail peered up at Lee. "You don't seem to like Tasker Scott. Why?"

"Among other things, he's the biggest crook unhung," Lee said succinctly. "As time will prove. Mister Vail, you hang on to your land. And tomorrow morning, should those hardcases show again, they'll probably run into a wild surprise."

Lee straightened up, crushed out the butt of his cigarette on his saddle horn. "I got things to do. Be seeing you folks again, shortly."

His glance went to Kip Vail again, and the swift brightness of her smile was something he carried away with him.

VII

"You figure your ride out to Carbide Junction was worthwhile?" Buck Theodore asked.

"I'll let you be the judge of that, Buck," Lee Cone answered.

They were gathered in the old line camp cabin on Laurel Creek—Lee, Buck, and Jack Dhu.

Jack, on directions from Lee, had ridden out to the place, introduced himself to Buck, explaining that he was to wait there with Buck until Lee got back from Carbide Junction. During the few days' interim, Jack and Buck had become well acquainted, knowing respect and liking for each other.

Jack Dhu had been a lone wolf most of his life, drifting from one job to another across a wide spread of country. It had been a hard life, many times holding to only a whisker's width inside the law. The loneliness had made him hard-shelled and aloof, and for years he had counted the gun at his hip his only real friend.

But now, in Lee Cone and Buck Theodore, Jack Dhu had found two men he liked and trusted. Here, in this little cabin, he knew a strange contentment he'd never hoped to find. He grinned at Lee.

"Go ahead and tell him, Lee. He's been itchy as an old pack rat."

"Well," Lee began to explain, "I got a look at some cattle shipping invoices at Carbide Junction. I didn't go through all that were there, but I looked over enough to serve my purpose. Buck, you told me you didn't know where the cattle Tasker Scott rustled went to. I'll tell you. They went out through Carbide Junction.

Flat T cattle, vented to Lazy Dollar. And . . ."

"What's that?" yelped Buck. "Flat T vented to Lazy Dollar! Why, I never sold a head of stock to Tasker Scott. Not a single damned head!"

"Of course you didn't," Lee said quietly, attempting to soothe Buck's rising temper. "Those vented brands were rustled stuff. There's no way you could blot a Flat T to Lazy Dollar and make it fool any inspector. So Scott just played it bold as brass. He vented, just like he'd bought the stuff on a regular, square deal. And here's the snapper on the whip. He had gall enough to sign his own name to the shipping invoices."

Jack Dhu whistled softly. "That man is either crazy, or figures he's too big to be touched."

"The last," Lee agreed, nodding. "He figured he had Buck licked, and he never expected me to show up again in Maacama Basin. He was wrong in both cases. And to top it all off, he hasn't got a bill of sale for any Flat T cattle to back his hand."

"Not only crazy," murmured Jack Dhu. "But a plain damned fool."

"No," Buck Theodore said slowly. "Not altogether, Jack. Call him slick and a gambler. And I was licked, just too tired and discouraged to care anymore. And Lee was gone, maybe dead, for all anybody here knew. Call it a gamble, and not as long as some that have got by. And also, he figured he was too big and had too much influence to be hit. Maybe he's right, there. What do you aim to do about it, Lee?"

"Choke him on the whole business," rapped Lee. "Here's something else." He went on to tell about the word of the railroad spur coming in through Smoky Pass. And he also told of the attempt to run the Vail family off their land.

"I promised John Vail our help," he ended. He studied the faces of Buck and Jack, before adding: "And we got to make that promise good. Buck, you and Jack roll up some blankets for yourselves and spend the night along the river near the Vails. If those two buckos, Stump and Pecos, show up acting nasty and threatening, you know what to do."

"Now that," said Buck with alacrity, "is something that sure appeals to me. Them two jiggers been holding down at the old home ranch like they owned it. I'll enjoy a chance to set 'em back on their heels. But where you aiming to be, boy, while the fun is going on?"

"I'll be around," Lee assured him. "But I got some things to do first. Starting with a shave. How's for a loan of your razor, Buck?"

VIII

The Lazy Dollar headquarters stood just where the more level land of the basin began to climb into the first slope of the Mineral Hills. Even back in the days when Pete Garland was alive, it had been the biggest spread in that part of the country.

The ranch house was big and solid and comfortable. Lee Cone rode up to it with some caution and a great deal of grimness. For sight of it brought back a lot of memories. Memories of evenings spent on the broad verandah with Lucy Garland and of the fine dreams he had fashioned there, as well as the memory of that bitter day when Lucy and Tasker Scott and Pete Garland had stood on that same verandah while Pete Garland had given him the word of Lucy's sudden marriage to Tasker Scott.

The place was quiet now. In an open-faced shed out by the corrals stood the shiny buggy Lucy had been driving the day Lee had come into town and seen her, so he figured she was home.

A moment later Lucy herself stepped from the ranch house door and came out to the edge of the porch. When he pulled up in front of the steps, she exclaimed with pleasure.

"Lee! I knew you'd come to see me."

He dismounted and looked at her gravely, knowing a small feeling of irritability. She still felt she held the old power over him, and just now he wasn't sure that she didn't. For the same old sultry, exciting dark beauty was there. He tried to keep his tone casual as he climbed the steps.

"I came because I had some things to tell you, Lucy. Things I'm afraid you won't enjoy hearing . . . especially from me."

She tilted her head and said with assurance: "I'm interested only in talking about us, Lee. Come on in."

Lee hesitated, but he needed to talk to her, so he followed her inside.

The living room was big and cool and shadowed. It had its memories, too.

Lucy turned abruptly, came close to him, put her hands on his arms, and stood staring up at him. She nodded.

"The same man. A little older, but the same man."

Lee shook his head, and his tone ran dry. "No, Lucy. The older part is right . . . but I'm not the same man. The Lee Cone you knew is one who belongs to the past. This is a different one."

"I don't believe it," she retorted. "There was always something steadfast about you, Lee. I was the wrong one. And if it's any satisfaction to you, I've paid . . . plenty!"

"Folks who try to play both ends against the middle generally do, Lucy."

He tried to move away from her, but she clung to him.

"No, Lee . . . no!" Then, before he could stop her, her arms had slid around his neck, she had pulled his head down, and her lips were warm and pulsing against his own.

For a moment he was blindly confused, and then a curious calm ran through him. For there was no sweetness for him here, only a cold distaste. And he knew in this moment that any lingering spell this woman had held for him was completely dead. This was not the person he'd once loved. This was another man's wife, a selfish woman whose only sense of values was her own personal desires. And the fervor of her kiss left him completely unmoved.

He pulled her arms from about his neck, held her away from him. "It won't do, Lucy. You're married, remember? You're Missus Tasker Scott."

She stared at him for a moment. Then she said: "Tasker Scott! I hate him. I despise him!"

Lee nodded. "That, I think, was inevitable from the first. But the fact remains that you're still his wife. And to me you're just another woman."

"I don't believe that, Lee. You're not the sort to change. . . ."

"Time changes many things," he cut in. "Circumstances, too. The old days are dead, Lucy."

She watched him intently, and then a hardness crept in about her mouth.

"If they are, why did you come to visit me?"

He twisted up a cigarette before answering, and then he spoke slowly through a haze of blue smoke. "Mainly, I came to tell you that I'm going after your husband."

"Going after Tasker! In what way?"

"I'm going to break him."

"Why?"

"Because," Lee said slowly, distinctly, "he's a crook. He's lied, thieved, and fattened himself on better men. He's taken things away from me and my friends. I'm going to take them back. Doing it, I'll be hurting you, too. I'll be sorry for that. I have no wish to hurt you, Lucy."

He watched the change come over her, watched that calculating hardness which reduced her natural beauty to a brittle shell that repelled him.

Abruptly she put back her head and laughed, and the laugh was as hard as her look.

"You find it funny?" Lee drawled.

"Very funny." She looked him up and down. "You . . . a rundown, drifting cowhand . . . talking of breaking Tasker Scott. Yes, that's very funny. Tasker may be all you say he is, but he's much too big for you to break him. You're a fool to think you even have a chance at that . . . a hopeless fool."

Lee might have been completely impervious

to her personal charms, but he was not to the scornful bite of her words.

"We'll see who is the hopeless fool," he retorted. "Ask your husband what kind of a fool would ship vented brands, and put his name on the shipping invoice, while not holding any sort of bill of sale for those vented brands. Ask the damned cow thief that!"

Then he turned and left the house.

She followed him out onto the porch, hating him now because he had rebuffed her, hating him because he saw through her so completely. Her voice was shrill as she called after him.

"You realize of course that when you fight Tasker, you fight me, too. For all that Tasker has is mine. And what is mine, I keep!"

It stood out in her now, naked and unashamed, the self-centered, calculating selfishness that had been the guiding spirit of her entire existence. It was the thing that had made her marry Tasker Scott in the first place. She had weighed him against Scott, measured them both with a calculating shrewdness, and decided that she saw in Scott a man able to furnish her with more of the world's goods. It was doubtful that she had ever really loved either of them; it was doubtful if she'd ever loved anyone but herself.

Just why she hated her husband, and had so bluntly said so, Lee didn't know. Perhaps the ruthlessness in her had clashed with the ruthlessness in Scott, and out of it had sprung a mutual hate.

Lee took a final drag on his cigarette, tossed the butt aside. "I'm sorry for you, Lucy," he said. "No matter what you think you have, you really haven't a thing in the world that really counts. Someday you'll understand that."

He walked over to his horse, swung into the saddle, and rode out of the yard.

Less than an hour later, Lucy Scott's shiny buggy whirled to a stop in front of her husband's office. Inside, Tasker Scott was talking to his two henchmen, Stump and Pecos, and in a far corner of the office, Braz Boland sat staring grumpily at the floor.

At Lucy's abrupt entrance Scott started up impatiently, but Lucy forestalled the words she saw coming.

"You'd better listen to me, Tasker. It's important."

He stared at her, then jerked a short nod. To Stump and Pecos he said: "You fellows know what to do. Make it stick!"

They went out, Stump looking at Lucy with an insolence that made her flush. To Boland, as he followed the other two, Scott said: "I'm giving you another chance, Boland. But if you let anybody take that badge off you again, you're finished."

Left alone with his wife, Scott turned. "Well?"

"I had a visitor out at the ranch," Lucy told him. "Lee Cone."

The jealous anger flared in Tasker Scott's eyes. "You'll taunt me once too often about that fellow. I'll stand for no sneaking behind my back. You or nobody else can make that kind of a fool out of me."

"Maybe you've been a fool in other ways. Did you ever ship any Flat T cattle, vented to Lazy Dollar?"

Tasker Scott's eyes narrowed. "I may have. Why should it concern you?"

"It doesn't, but it better concern you. Because Lee Cone knows about it. He also knows that you have no bill of sale to cover those Flat T cattle and that you were stupid enough to have your name on the shipping invoices."

Tasker Scott lowered himself slowly in his desk chair, got out a cigar, and lighted up. "Cone told you this?"

"That, and more. He said he was going to break you, and if he's got that kind of evidence, he's liable to."

"Why should he have told you that?"

Lucy shrugged. "Because in his way he's a fool, too. He said he was going to break you, and that he knew I'd be hurt, too. That part of it he professed to regret, though why I can't understand."

Tasker Scott sneered. "Still in love with you, my dear. Still hoping."

"No," said Lucy curtly. "He's not in love with me at all. But men like Lee Cone have a sense of honor that people like you and I can't figure out. We live on one level, he's on another. And it is a considerably higher level than ours."

Scott sneered again. "Now you're getting sentimental. Did you see any of those invoices that you spoke of?"

"No. But Lee must have, or he wouldn't have had the wording so pat. They exist, don't they? And that wipes out my last shred of respect for you, which was respect for your shrewdness."

Scott did not flare at this. Instead, he rolled his cigar about in his mouth, then took a deep drag on it and peered with narrowed eyes through the smoke.

"I'm trying to figure out why you bothered to bring me the word?"

"Because your business affairs are *my* business affairs. What you have is *mine,* too. And what is taken away from you is *my* loss," she paused to let that sink in. "Well, I've warned you," she added before turning and heading out the door before he could say another word.

Tasker Scott stayed as he was, scowling through the smoke. A thread of uneasiness stirred in him. How had Lee Cone found out about those invoices? And had he set any forces of authority to work? What could Scott do now to save himself?

The answer came to him with hard, abrupt impact. He still felt he had nothing really to fear from Buck Theodore, especially if Buck was alone, for Buck had reached the age when no fight was worth it. But Lee Cone! There was the sticker . . . Lee Cone.

Tasker Scott got up and went to a rear door of his office, which opened into the warehouse, and yelled a man's name.

When the man appeared, he listened to Scott's order, nodded, and went away.

Scott himself went over to a heavy iron safe in a corner of the room, opened it, and, glancing around before he did so, pulled out a cash drawer. From this he counted out some currency. He went back to his desk, split the bills into two equal amounts, put each of these into separate envelopes, and sealed them. Then he touched a match to his cigar and waited.

It was nearly an hour later before Stump and Pecos came in.

Stump looked at Tasker Scott inquiringly and grumbled: "What's the idea . . . change of plans?"

Tasker Scott nodded. "For the present, yes. That granger out at the foot of Smoky Pass is the least of my troubles now. So he can wait. But this fellow Cone we talked about before . . . you'd know him if you saw him again?"

They both nodded.

"We'd know him," Pecos affirmed. "We got a good look at him that day he was out at the ranch, when he was asking about Buck Theodore."

"Wish I'd known he was going out there that day," Scott said harshly. "I could have tipped you boys off. You could have closed out a lot of trouble for me, right on the spot. As it is"—he indicated the two envelopes sitting on his desk—"there's two hundred and fifty dollars in each of these. The day Lee Cone turns up dead, you fellows can each pick up one of the envelopes." He paused to look at the two thoughtfully. "Well?" he asked.

They glanced at the envelopes, and then steadied their eyes on Scott.

A small, feral spark shone in Stump's eyes. "Getting troublesome, this fellow Cone?"

"Plenty!" snapped Scott.

"How, when, and where?" Pecos droned nasally.

"Any way, any time, any place," Tasker Scott responded. "And the quicker the better."

Stump grinned wolfishly.

IX

John Vail had left his heavy wagon at the spot of his original camp, as indication of ownership of the quarter section he'd filed on, but he'd moved a lot of his equipment down to the more comfortable camp beside the river.

The afternoon was running out when Lee Cone rode in there.

Buck Theodore and Jack Dhu had already arrived, made themselves acquainted with the Vails, and explained why they were there. Buck Theodore had already won the hearts of the two Vail youngsters, his pocketknife busy with a piece of soft pine driftwood, fashioning all sorts of amazing things dear to the hearts of a small boy and girl.

Jack Dhu was squatted on his heels, smoking, watching John Vail mend a bit of harness. Mrs. Vail and Kip were busy about the supper fire, but as soon as she saw Lee, she straightened to face Lee with open gladness.

Lee had become supremely conscious of this young woman. He was particularly so now, after the distasteful memories of what he had left behind him at the Lazy Dollar headquarters. There he'd found deceit, dishonesty, and hateful spite. Here was the direct opposite. It was like

76

meeting a clean, sweet wind after climbing out of some dank lowland.

He walked closer to the fire. Mrs. Vail had moved a little way apart from the fire and this gave Lee a chance to speak to Kip and say exactly what he felt. He kept his voice low.

"There is such loveliness in you, Kip. I realize it more each time I see you."

An honest, warm color ran up her cheeks and a soft smile touched her lips. Her answer was a murmur he could barely hear.

"If you do, I'm glad, Lee."

She turned back to the fire and her cooking.

Lee moved back to his horse which he unsaddled and picketed in a handy little meadow along with Buck's and Jack Dhu's mounts. When he returned, Buck had finished his whittling and joined John Vail and Jack Dhu. Lee went over to them.

"No further sign of those two hardcases," reported John Vail. "If they show up now, they'll run into a wild surprise. Sure white of you fellows to stand ready to give me a hand."

"In a way it's a common cause, Mister Vail," Lee told him.

A little later Mrs. Vail announced supper, and Lee and Buck and Jack Dhu managed a few words alone before going over to the fire.

Buck looked at Lee keenly. "Been guessing to

myself where you been all afternoon, boy. Think I hit the answer. A fire is out, or it ain't. Well?"

"Completely out, Buck," Lee told him quietly. "The ashes are stone cold. I wonder now that there was ever any fire. But I felt I had to tell her that I was going to smash her husband. I wanted her to know it was him I was fighting, not her."

Buck pinched his pursed lips with thumb and forefinger. "Not too sure that was wise, boy. She's sure to tell her husband, and that means he'll be forewarned and set out to do things of his own."

Lee shrugged. "He would have in any event. The attempt by Boland to arrest me proves it. Tasker Scott's hand was plain to see. It doesn't matter. I want him to know it. I want him to sweat."

They ate supper with the Vails, while the sun went down and the soft, blue dusk came stealing in. In the background the river waters splashed restfully over the shallows, sparrows twittered sleepily in the willows, and from an alder top a lone oriole sang the day into darkness.

Buck and Jack Dhu had spread their blankets downstream from the Vail camp and Buck had brought an extra bedroll for Lee. So they lounged on these, smoking, silent for the most part with their own thoughts.

Once, Jack Dhu stirred and mumbled in his sleep quietly.

• • •

It was a quiet night and Lee Cone slept the good sleep of a man with no regrets over the past and only high hopes and purpose for the future. He was up at daylight and went softly over to the river shallows to wash up. He could see a slim figure there ahead of him.

Kip's face was rosy from the chill bite of the water and from the vigorous toweling that followed. Now she was seated on a rock, brushing her hair. She showed just a touch of confusion at sight of Lee.

"You're a light sleeper, Kip," he said teasingly.

"No," she said, in that rich, husky voice. "It isn't that. It's just that I love the time when day first breaks. Everything is so vital and cool and clean. The birds are awake and celebrating. It makes me want to celebrate, too. Isn't that silly?"

"Not a bit," declared Lee. "I know just how you feel. Early morning and twilight . . . the best times of the day as far as I'm concerned."

Lee splashed and sputtered as he doused his face and head with water, making Kip laugh softly as she tossed him her towel.

"You remind me of my little brother. All the huffing and puffing over a little face washing."

Lee used the towel gratefully, grinning at her as he scrubbed the towel all over his head, imagining he could smell her on it. Then, as he handed back the towel, he captured her hand, held it.

Kip came to her feet, went very still, her eyes clear and wide and searching. She saw what was in Lee's eyes, and she whispered: "Not unless you mean it, Lee."

"I never meant anything more in my life," Lee told her soberly. "I'm as sure of that as I am that we are both alive."

He drew her to him and kissed her, and her lips were sweet.

After a few moments she drew back from him, stood looking at him. And the smile that she gave him held the gentlest glory he'd ever seen. Then she turned and hurried back to camp.

Lee followed along presently and got the fire going. The crackle of it brought the rest of the camp alive.

Mrs. Vail, making coffee, shook the can. "Not enough for another day," she declared. "And we could use another side of bacon and a sack of flour, too. I told you, John Vail, that we should have stocked up with more supplies when we were in Antelope. But you were in such a howling hurry to get out to our piece of land. . . ."

"I know, Mary," said Vail. "I got to get a new tent, too. So we'll hitch up the wagon and drive into town today and get everything we need."

Vail announced his intention to Lee and Buck and Jack Dhu as they gathered around the breakfast fire.

"The land will be here when we get back," he ended. "I've filed according to law, and nobody can say different."

"Couldn't somebody jump your claim while we're away, Dad?" asked Kip.

Jack Dhu showed her a grave, small smile. "They do, miss, and they'll jump right off again. You can be sure of that."

Kip Vail hadn't been entirely sure just how to take this saddle man at first. But now, suddenly, she liked and trusted him. She smiled.

"Now that I think of it, I'm quite sure they would," she agreed.

While John Vail was hooking his team to his wagon, Buck Theodore drew Lee aside. "Where do we go from here, boy?"

"Town," Lee answered. "To sort of keep an eye on the Vails, just in case those two hardcase riders of Tasker Scott's should run into them and get any ideas. Then, I want to see Scott himself and lay the chips on the table. Did some thinking about it last night. He may have rustled you blind, Buck . . . but he got title to the ranch according to law, and that's the main thing I want to get back. When we get that, we have a foundation to build on again. Without the ranch and the range, we got nothing."

"You mean you aim to try and make some sort of deal with him?" demanded Buck.

Lee nodded slowly. "Guess you'd call it that. He transfers title of the ranch back to us and pays us a fair price for the cattle he rustled, and then I don't press the rustling charge. Otherwise, I see him behind bars . . . or dead."

Buck frowned worriedly. "You think he'll deal?"

"He'll have his choice." Lee shrugged. "It's up to him."

Lucy Scott faced a new day with an apathy that left her wan and subdued. She had spent the night alone in the big ranch house, her husband not having come home at any point during the night. It had been the longest night in her memory and she had done a lot of thinking, and had known one period of sudden, unaccountable tears. And that had been highly unsettling, too, for she wasn't easily given to tears.

Over and over, during the night, Lee Cone's words had come back to her.

No matter what you think you have, you really haven't a thing in the world. . . .

She had gotten up and paced back and forth, angrily denying the truth of this, telling herself that she was rich, that she had everything. But deep inside her there persisted a stubborn realization that Lee Cone had spoken the truth. It was when she finally admitted the fact to herself that she had broken down and wept.

She knew neither love or respect for Tasker Scott, and he had none for her. Their marriage had been a mockery from the first. It had amassed the worldly goods she had thought she wanted, much of them gained through trickery, slick dealing, and deceit—even outright robbery, such as the rustling of the Flat T cattle. But now such goods had no appeal for her, and she hated them as she hated herself and the man she had married.

She thought of the old days when she and Lee Cone had ridden together, danced together, built big dreams together. There had been true happiness right in the hollow of her hand, and she had reached for the glitter of gold instead.

"But there's good in me," she whimpered to herself. "I know there's some good in me. There must be."

It was a cruel awakening Lucy Scott came to during those distraught hours. But it did come, and out of it truth emerged. There was only one thing she could do that would ever bring her real peace of mind again.

She could see to it that all the real possessions that had been taken away from Lee Cone and Buck Theodore were returned to them. Their ranch, the value of their cattle. All these must go back to them. A great peace came to her as she reached this decision.

She went to the door of the house, called across to a ranch hand, ordered her buggy and team made ready. Then she washed and dressed, and once she was in the buggy, she drove swiftly off along the town road. She knew a bitter scene lay ahead when she faced her husband with the demand she was about to make. But her head was high.

The John Vail wagon rolled to a stop in front of Asa Bingham's store. At the far end of the hitch rail, Lee Cone, Jack Dhu, and Buck Theodore dismounted and secured their horses. Buck watched the Vails get down off the wagon and go into the store, the two youngsters round-eyed and excited at this visit to town. The old cattleman grinned.

"I'm going in and buy those two kids some hard candy," he announced.

Jack Dhu dropped on his heels against the front of the store and built a smoke. "As good a place as any to keep an eye on things," he said laconically. "Just in case that four-flusher of a marshal, Braz Boland, should show again. Unless you want me along with you, Lee?"

Lee shook his head. "I can handle Tasker Scott all right."

Traffic along the street was a little less hectic than usual and Lee cut across toward Tasker Scott's office. He felt good this morning. For one thing, several matters he hadn't been sure of in the past were now entirely settled in his mind. He knew that he was completely free of the old lure Lucy Scott had once held for him. He had ferreted out evidence with which to force Tasker Scott's hand. And he had found a sure answer to the loneliness he had known in the touch of Kip Vail's lips and the soft glory in her eyes. Yeah, the world and its future were looking up.

In an eating house along the street, Tasker Scott's men, Stump and Pecos, had just finished a late breakfast. Stump, chewing on a tooth pick, moved to the door of the place while Pecos settled up with the waitress. Stump's glance at the street, casual at first, abruptly became a fixed, hot stare, and his voice was a quick, hard rasp across his shoulder.

"Pecos, get out here. Quick!"

Pecos hurried to Stump's side. "There goes our money," he said, pointing in Cone's direction. "We'll never have a better chance."

As they broke out onto the plank walk-way, Pecos reminded Stump: "We're in town, remember. We can't make it too raw."

"I'll give him the yell," said Stump. "When he turns around, we'll move in on him. He'll be looking at us when he gets it. Scott can do the arguing, after."

• • •

In his office, Tasker Scott showed the effects of a hard night. Instead of going out to the Lazy Dollar headquarters for the night, he'd taken a room in the hotel, where he kept company with a whiskey bottle till three a.m. As a rule, he wasn't a heavy drinker, but that was before Lee Cone had returned to Maacama Basin. And since he knew what Lee Cone had found out about the shipments of the rustled Flat T cattle, he was beset by nervousness and, at times, a feeling of doom.

Knowledge that he had slipped badly had set him to wondering if he hadn't left some loopholes in other shady deals. The more he thought of these things, the more his imagination got out of control. He began seeing threats everywhere. And he had taken that whiskey bottle to his room with him in an attempt to quiet his nagging fears.

True, he had set Stump and Pecos after Cone. But in a thing of that sort, you could never be sure. He had set up Braz Boland as marshal to get Cone out of circulation, and that hadn't worked at all. Maybe this other try would fall flat, too. No, a man could never be sure of hirelings. If he wanted a job done right, he often had to do it himself.

Tasker Scott slid a hand under his coat to his left armpit, felt the butt of the gun in the shoulder holster there. If he had to, would he be able to reach for that gun and face it out with Lee Cone?

He licked his lips, got his desk bottle out of a drawer, took another pull at it. The whiskey was raw and harsh against his already queasy stomach, and his lips pulled thin in a grimace. His eyes were heavy and bloodshot, and his nerves were beginning to jerk at him again.

Lee Cone hit the board sidewalk some twenty yards from the door of Tasker Scott's office. Here the false front of a saloon lifted, and from the door of the saloon, Braz Boland stepped. He was wearing his marshal's badge again, and now he stopped, dead still, face to face with Lee Cone.

Lee stopped, alert for anything, and his words hit out at Boland.

"I'm looking at you this time, Boland, so don't try anything! That badge you're wearing doesn't mean a thing to me."

Braz Boland was startled and discomfited. He'd taken a savage tongue-lashing from Tasker Scott over the mess he'd made on his first attempt to arrest Cone, and he'd been telling himself ever since that he wouldn't fumble the next chance.

But now he knew that it had been a false courage that had been talking. Face to face with the man he had grown to hate so blackly, Boland realized he didn't have what it took. For there was something about Lee Cone just now. . . .

Boland turned and went back into the saloon.

Lee Cone went on, and was within ten strides of the door of Tasker Scott's office when a harsh yell hit at him from behind.

"Cone! This way, Cone!"

Lee whirled. Fifty yards away, and closing in on him, were Stump and Pecos. Where they'd come from, Lee had no idea, but there was no mistaking their intent. It stood out all over them, ugly and uncompromising. These two were on the kill!

Stump's harsh yell had reached other ears than those of Lee Cone. In front of Asa Bingham's store, Jack Dhu's head jerked up. It took only a glance to tell Jack what was in the air, for he was an old hand at this sort of business. With one lithe lunge he was on his feet and running.

The wall of Tasker Scott's big warehouse was at Lee Cone's back. To his left, a few short strides away, was the door of Scott's office. For a moment Lee thought of making a dash for that door, but immediately he knew this would do him no good. There was nothing he could do about it but see it through, take his chance of one against two. This was show-down time.

He spread his feet, crouched slightly, and fixed his glance on Stump and Pecos with bitter intensity. He thought to himself: *Let them make the first move, and then . . .*

Down at the far end of the street a shining

buggy, drawn by a fast-stepping team of matched bay horses, rolled into view. Lucy Scott had arrived in town.

Lee Cone didn't see the buggy or its occupant. He saw nothing but the two gunfighters advancing so remorselessly on him. Every ounce of concentration in him was centered on those two. He scrubbed the open palm of his right hand up and down on the leg of his jeans.

Jack Dhu was swearing softly to himself as he ran. If he could just have been at Lee's side at this moment. But he wasn't. He was long, long yards away. Yet, there was one break he could win for Lee. He drew his gun and, when he saw Stump and Pecos come to a stop, spread a little apart, and go into a slight forward lean, Jack Dhu shoved his gun forward and sent the first hard snarl of report boiling along the street.

Jack hadn't expected to hit at this range, especially while on the run. He hadn't hoped to. All he wanted to do was startle the two gunfighters, to throw them off balance. But he shot closer than he realized.

The slug had crashed into the holstered gun at Stump's right hip, and the shock of it staggered Stump and spun him half around.

It broke Pecos into bewildered action, too. He dragged his gun, then hung in a moment of indecision as to whether to cut down on Lee

Cone or turn to face this unexpected danger from behind. In the middle of that fatal second, Lee Cone's gun pounded heavily.

Lee had seized on the break Jack Dhu's shot had given him. He saw Stump spin under the impact of Jack's bullet, and threw his own lead squarely into the center of Pecos's lank middle.

Pecos gasped at the impact, jack-knifed, and fell forward.

Stump, cat-fast in spite of his unwieldy bulk, recovered his balance, grabbed for his gun, felt the torn holster leather, the split and battered butt of the weapon, then dropped to one knee and caught up the gun Pecos had dropped.

Stump ducked completely under Lee's second shot, made his try at Lee a little too hurriedly, and missed by a hair.

That was when Braz Boland stepped from the saloon door and cut down deliberately on Lee from the side.

It was as though someone had swung a massive blow against Lee's right shoulder. He spun into the wall behind him and went down, and both Boland and Stump, firing again as he went down, missed that falling target.

Out in the middle of the street, close enough now to be sure, Jack Dhu came to a halt and threw two lightning fast shots—one at Stump, the other at Braz Boland. This was one business Jack Dhu understood thoroughly. He struck like a wolf might strike, with the same awful, deadly speed.

Stump, seeing Lee go down, was whirling to meet the threat from behind. Halfway through the move a savage force seemed to pick him up and shake him. Then he fell, landing on his face.

On his part, Braz Boland went loose all over. He took two backward steps, then fell through the saloon doors, leaving them winnowing wildly back and forth, with only Boland's boots showing beneath the door.

In his office, Tasker Scott had jerked out of his chair at the sound of that first shot. He ran to the office door, swung it open. He saw Pecos die, he saw Stump die, and saw Braz Boland die. And he saw Lee Cone down, half sitting, half lying. But Lee Cone wasn't dead. On the contrary, he had caught up his gun in his left hand, and was struggling to his knees.

The movement at the door of Scott's office caught Lee's eye. He looked and saw Tasker Scott there, and Scott was just beginning to reach inside his coat for his shoulder-holster gun. Scott was cursing without sense or meaning, and he was throwing down on Lee.

Lee pushed his gun out and the recoil of it drove his elbow back.

Sudden paralysis seemed to strike Tasker Scott.

Any movement in him stilled. Then he slid down into a sitting position in the doorway of his office and his head sagged forward. He looked like a man dozing, or sunk in deep meditation. His head dropped lower and lower while all substance seemed to melt out of him. Then he was just a crumpled, lifeless bulk.

Lee Cone rocked back and forth on his knees, staring blindly at nothing.

X

Lee came back to earth out of a nightmare of pain due to the smell of the iodoform. He swore weakly at a burly doctor for hurting him. The doctor merely grinned in response and caused him pain again when he stuck a needle of some kind into him. After that, he slept.

He awakened in a shadowed room, feeling weak and puny, but otherwise fairly good, except for his right shoulder, which hurt with a throbbing, devilish persistence. Occasionally a gray-haired woman appeared who fed him a thin broth and made him take pills. Then he would sleep again.

It went on like that for days, it seemed, though each time he awoke the pain in his shoulder was less severe.

Finally, one day when he opened his eyes, it was to see Buck Theodore and Jack Dhu.

"Where you jiggers been?" demanded Lee in a weak anger.

"Handy all the time, boy," answered Buck. "You scared the hell out of us. Recollect what happened?"

Lee nodded. "Rotten mess, wasn't it?"

"Cleared the air a heap though," Jack Dhu assured Lee. "We didn't ask for it, Lee . . . they did. Don't go to brooding about it."

Lee looked up. "You saved my skin, Jack."

Jack's answering smile was faint, but it warmed up his face immensely. "You did all right yourself. But don't you worry about nothing for now. Just you hurry and get well, so I can enjoy myself cussing you. Now you two got things to talk about. I'll be around later."

Jack moved away and the door closed softly.

Buck Theodore moved in closer to the bed, commenting: "There goes one damned good man, boy. Sure glad he's going to stay on with us out at the ranch."

"The ranch? We ain't got no ranch, Buck. Now that Tasker Scott's dead, we can't make no deal for it."

Buck sat on the edge of the bed. "We got our ranch back, Lee. And a check for all the cattle Scott rustled from us. Lucy Scott saw to that." Buck let that sink in before he continued. "When things quieted down again after that ruckus, Lucy sent for me. She handed me the deed to our old spread and a check for the cattle. Said she wanted to right some of the wrongs she felt she was equally responsible for with Tasker Scott. We're all set for the future, boy."

Lee lay quiet for some time. Finally he stirred a little. "How did she seem to feel about what happened to . . . Tasker?"

Buck shrugged. "Got a lot more courage than I thought she had, Lucy has. I've been doing a lot of apologizing to myself for things I've thought and said about her. A strain of pretty good color showed up in her when the chips were down. She's gone away on a long trip. I doubt she'll ever come back, for I understand she's left all her affairs in the hands of the banker to liquidate for her."

"Wherever she is," Lee said softly, mostly to himself, "I wish her luck."

"Speaking of luck," said Buck. "You got more than you deserve, young fellow. It's waiting right outside the door of this room."

Buck gave Lee a small squeeze on his good shoulder and scurried out of the room.

Lee twisted his head at the sound of a soft step and watched as Kip Vail crossed over to his bed. And by the look on her face he knew that Buck was certainly right about his luck.

She stood for a moment looking down at him. Then she dropped on her knees beside the bed, put her face in her hands, and started to cry.

"That terrible day," she whispered brokenly. "I . . . I saw it all from the door of the store. Those . . . those guns hammering. Men going down . . . and you one of them. Oh, Lee . . . Lee!"

With his sound left hand he patted her tear-wet cheek. "Anything that brought you to me is worth it, Kip," he told her gently.

Presently she got up and sat on the bed.

He smiled at her. "Lot of good dawns to face together. I'm thinking of one dawn right now . . . just you and me beside the river. Remember?"

She leaned low and kissed him. "I remember," she murmured.

THE DESERT RIDER

I

"Do you really think he will come, Uncle Jack?"

Sheriff Jack Carleton nodded. "I reckon he will, Donna. Folks do say Buck English is kinda chary about givin' his word to anything. But when he does give it . . . it's as good as an oath. He never breaks it."

They were in Jack Carleton's office in Cedarville. Through the open door the sunlight glimmered in dazzling reflection from the white, powdery dust of the street. It was two hours past midday and for those entire two hours Donna Carleton had been sitting there beside her uncle, waiting for Buck English.

Donna's face, in repose, was not in accord with the accepted standards of feminine beauty. Her mouth was too wide and her chin was too strong. But there was character there—character and strength and a certain softly brooding wisdom.

From a Spanish mother, who had died at the girl's birth, Donna had inherited a silken crown of sleek, blue-black hair and dusky, warm coloring. From her father, who had been Jack Carleton's elder brother, she had gotten a pair of level blue eyes and her forceful chin and mouth. She was of medium height, slender—free-limbed as a boy. Perhaps her greatest charm lay in the

99

aura of sparkling health and well-being which surrounded her. She was the apple of her uncle's eye.

"You know," she said thoughtfully, "I've always heard that you would gamble on anything, Uncle Jack. But it seems to me that this idea concerning Buck English is the longest chance you ever took. To put a man of his reputation in charge of our ranch looks almost like inviting a wolf to look after some lambs."

Jack Carleton chuckled. "You're bound and determined to make Buck out a no-good scalawag, ain't you, honey? Mebbe you'll be surprised."

"But," argued the girl, "you've told me yourself that Buck English is wild . . . that he's killed men . . . that he is liable to step beyond the law at any time. And, knowing what a stickler you are for law and order . . . well, it just seems queer to me."

"I'll grant you that I've said that about Buck. It's the truth. Only . . . he ain't exactly got beyond the law yet. But he's liable to at any time. And there ain't nothin' I'd hate any worse than havin' to go out and get Buck . . . I mean, put the cuffs on him and bring him in." The sheriff paused briefly to shift in his chair.

"You know . . . Buck's daddy used to be sheriff of this county. There never walked or breathed a squarer, finer, gamer man than Martin English.

He was my friend . . . and your daddy's friend. And Martin English caught and brought to justice the men who killed your daddy. Sure we both owe the English clan somethin' for that.

"I was with Martin English when he died . . . from a slug that caught him in the back by a dirty rat who wasn't fit to lick his boots. At the time Martin didn't say so, but I know his last thought and hope was that Buck would make a worthwhile man of himself. The kid ain't had a great deal of chance to do it yet. I admit he's been runnin' kinda wild. But he worshiped his daddy and his dad's death sorta broke him all to pieces. He flew off at a tangent, you might say. I'm hopin' to drag him back to travelin' the safety of a straight line. The best way I know of doin' it is to give him work and responsibility. That's why I intend to offer him the job. And somethin' tells me I ain't gamblin' a bit, either. I got a hunch the kid will make good."

Donna smiled, before she repeated: "Kid! Kid! To hear you talk Uncle Jack, one would imagine Buck English hadn't reached voting age yet."

"Well, by my calculatin' he ain't far past it, at that," said the sheriff, tamping tobacco into a black, stubby pipe.

Jack Carleton was a sparely built man of middle age, with a thin face and blue eyes set deep beneath shaggy brows. His somewhat thin hair was sandy in color, as was the drooping mustache that bracketed his stern mouth.

"He ain't a day over twenty-five, if my memory serves me correct. Just a kid . . . a sick and sad kid."

"Sick!" exclaimed Donna.

"Mentally sick," confirmed the sheriff as his thoughts seemed to drift off for a few seconds. Then he nodded and continued: "See, Donna, it's like this. Physically Buck would pass as a high-grade young tiger anywhere. Like I said . . . his daddy's death broke Buck all up. It give him the wrong slant on things . . . made him bitter and hard . . . hard as flint. And when a twenty-five year ole kid gets that way . . . well, he's sick. Why if he was normal for his age, he'd be laughin' his way through life, fallin' in and out of love at every jump, crowdin' in on dances and parties and things of that sort.

"They tell me Buck won't even look at a woman. He drinks a little, gambles the same, and will fight a buzz saw at the drop of the hat. He's throwed his guns and got his man twice . . . in self-defense. But that's an unhealthy life for a boy his age. I'm gonna shake him outta it or know the reason why. And I expect you to help me, honey."

Donna's eyebrows lifted. "How can I help? I never dreamed I'd be asked to play the part of guardian to a rapidly developing bad man."

"Nobody is askin' that of you. What I want you to do is just act natural with Buck . . . same as you do the rest of the boys around here. Accept him like he was any other nice, clean-cut youngster. Smile at him, talk with him, ride with him. I reckon that'll take the tough edges off of him quicker than anything else."

Sheriff Carleton stopped at the sound of a horse outside. "Well, that there must be him coming in now."

Carleton jumped to his feet and went to the open door, where he stood waiting.

Donna was slower to get up and join her uncle. But as she leaned out around him, she caught a glimpse of a rider just jogging to a stop in front of the office. Suddenly a little panic gripped her, and Donna Carleton was not easily stampeded. She felt almost as though she was being called upon to face a wolf of some sort. To hide her agitation she walked over to the side window of the office, from which she could see the boldly jutting rim of Red Mesa, five miles to the south.

She heard her uncle call a greeting as he stepped out onto the plank walkway to which was given a deep answer in a flat, repressed voice. Boot heels clumped on the low steps and spur chains clashed musically. Donna turned slowly.

Her uncle had stepped aside and there, framed in the doorway, was a tall, wide-shouldered figure in faded blue shirt, flaring bat-wing chaps, and dusty, worn boots. Cartridge belts criss-crossed lean hips to end up in a pair of big, walnut-butted guns, jutting from open topped Mexican-style holsters.

A brief handclasp passed between the two men before Jack Carleton turned and waved his hand.

"Have a seat, Buck. Oh yeah . . . meet Donna, my niece. Donna . . . this is Buck English."

The rider pulled off his hat and bowed stiffly. For a fractional second his eyes met Donna's and the sheriff's niece felt as though she had been shot through with icicles. She forced a smile she did not feel as she murmured an answer to his curt: "Glad to know you, Miss Carleton."

Carleton slid a chair over to his visitor, then sat down himself.

"Buck," said the sheriff abruptly, "I got a proposition to offer you. Things ain't been goin' any too well out at my Red Mesa Ranch. Sundown Sloan, who's been roddin' for me, is a good man. But he's gettin' along in years. He ain't able to ride as much as he used to and some of the boys have been takin' advantage of it. They ain't hittin' the ball like they should. Sundown come to me about it and asked for me to take the responsibility off of his shoulders and put it on a pair of younger, stronger ones. Right away I thought of you. I'd sure admire to have you take the job. How about it?"

The rider was plainly a little taken back by the

abruptness of the offer. He hesitated a moment, before answering. "Why . . . sure . . . that's mighty handsome of you, Jack . . . to think of me," he said, his voice still that deep, queerly repressed tone. "It's a royal chance for a fellow my age. But ain't you takin' quite a gamble? What makes you think I could handle it?"

"I knew your father," Carleton said quietly. "You're a lot like him in most ways, Buck. And he was the most capable man I ever knew. Also . . . I reckon it'd make him mighty proud, Buck . . . if he knew his boy was foreman of a spread like the Red Mesa Ranch."

Buck English was still for some time. Donna covertly studied him. His face was lean and brown and looked as hard as granite. There was power in that face. It told of a man who would never vacillate between good and bad. He would either be straight as a string or something awesomely malignant. His shadowed eyes gleamed that same brilliant, cold gray—inscrutable—piercing.

There was a boyish cast to his head, heightened in effect by the slightly curly brown hair that clung close to the contours of his skull. His brow was high, the brow of a thinker. There was force, almost ruthlessness in his arched nose and tightly clipped jaw. It was the mouth that made him appear older than his years, however—bitter, slightly twisted—sardonic.

Presently he spoke again. "I can't help wonderin', Jack . . . whether you're offerin' me this job because you really figure I can straighten out your spread . . . or whether you think it'll be the right sort of thing to keep me out of trouble."

The sheriff smiled slightly. "Both, Buck," he admitted. "You're old enough to know what the kinda pace you're goin' always leads to. Sooner or later you step over the edge. The law was one of the most sacred things in your daddy's existence, boy. He slaved for it . . . gave up his life for it in fact. He . . ."

"That's right," grated English harshly. "He gave up his life for it . . . for a damned cowardly law that sent him unarmed to gather in those yellow-backed snakes. Nobody knows what the law did to my dad better than I do. A bunch of whining dollar mongrels stripped him of his guns. It hurt business, they said, to have a sheriff take on the hard nuts in their ten-cent town and rock 'em off. Gun play had to stop.

"They made him go after his man with nothin' but his bare hands. So . . . a coyote who wouldn't have dared stay in the same county with him, had Dad been packing a gun . . . shoots him in the back, never givin' him a ghost of a chance. So much for your law. I got nothin' but contempt for such a law, Jack. You'll have to use some other kind of argument."

He was breathing hard as he finished, his lean,

muscular hands clenched, his mouth more twisted and bitter than ever.

"You've spoke the truth, Buck," Carleton drawled quietly, "but that don't change the facts. Every man must have some purpose in life . . . some ideal that shapes his thoughts and actions. If he ain't got it . . . he's not a man. He's a clod. Man to man, I can understand your feelin's and I can't blame you a lot. But it comes right down to what would have pleased your dad more than anythin' else." Carleton paused to let his words penetrate the son of his good friend.

"He was your ideal . . . and I reckon you were his pride," he finally picked up. "You sure owe somethin' to both them ideas. And you won't be payin' the debt by hellin' around and finally runnin' foul of the very law your dad gave his life for. It's up to you to make your choice, Buck. I don't know of a man who I thought more of than your dad . . . and I've always thought a lot of you. But I'm givin' it to you straight that, if it becomes necessary, I'll go out after you . . . and get you, just as quick as I would any other man. I wouldn't want to, understand . . . but I'd do it just the same. For you see, Buck, I'm the same kind of a fool about the law that your dad was. Think it over."

English did, for some time. A twisted smile gripped his lips as he looked up.

"Should I take you up on your proposition,

Jack . . . I hope it wouldn't be because you thought I was scared of that last threat."

"Oh, you danged stiff-necked young chump!" exploded Carleton. "Of course not. I never saw an English that was afraid of anythin'. That's just the trouble. If you'd get a little shaky over somethin' once in a while, you'd be easier to handle. No, kid . . . I'm not tryin' to threaten you or bully you in any way. I'm just makin' you an offer and paradin' some facts to prove you oughta take it."

English drew a deep breath. "¡*Bueno*! I'll do it, Jack."

The sheriff's thin face split in a joyous grin. The two men stood up and gripped hands.

Carleton knew the supreme success of a worthwhile victory; English the passing of futility and thwarted purpose, and the presence of something substantial in life at last. Each was richer.

"When can you go out to the ranch and take hold, Buck?" asked the sheriff.

"Soon as I can get there. I got my war bag out on my horse. Do I get it right that I can use my own methods in startin' the wheels turnin', Jack?"

"As long as you don't throw a gun. Of course that shouldn't be necessary. I reckon there's one or two cowpunchers out there that'll need a little tamin'. I ain't been able to give much attention to the place. This office takes just about all my time. Donna can ride out with you and she'll give you a better picture of conditions than I can.

"You can handle things just as though it was your own spread. You know . . . it's a devil of a note when the sheriff of a county can't even keep his own ranch runnin' on an even keel, ain't it? But either the ranch or the office has to be neglected and folks have been sorta demandin' results from this here office. So you see how it is. Good luck, Buck."

Donna had not anticipated the sudden suggestion of her uncle that she accompany Buck English out to the Red Mesa Ranch. Consequently, before she could frame an adequate excuse, the opportunity was gone.

She was a little uncertain about this lean, hard-jawed young cowpuncher, with the icy, dispassionate eyes. His presence affected her strangely. She was not exactly afraid of him, but a certain, queer, inexplicable timidity seized her, making her feel self-conscious and disturbed.

As they jogged out of Cedarville, Donna knew that many pairs of curious eyes followed them. A good majority of those eyes belonged to people Donna knew, and it required a distinct effort on her part to answer nods and words of recognition.

As for her companion, he seemed splendidly

unconcerned. He rode in an easy slouch, his eyes straight ahead and thoughtful. That he was also recognized and the object of speculation, apparently bothered him not at all. With his horse, his gun, and his own particular brand of independence, he seemed coldly self-sufficient.

Neither of them spoke until town lay a good mile behind them. Directly ahead the blazing rim of Red Mesa was etched boldly against the sky. Already the narrow trail had taken an upward trend, a climb that would endure for five long miles and grow steeper with each foot of progress. In the end it would top that distant wild rim, to wind another eight miles back to the southwest extremity of the mesa, where the ranch lay.

Beyond that spread the Tonto Desert, a red, fiery gulf of thirsty desolation. And still farther on, almost a hundred miles away, rose the twin peaks of the Madrigals, hazy, blue, haunting with wild allure.

It was Buck who broke the silence.

"Just what seems to be the main trouble out at the ranch, Miss Carleton?" he asked quietly.

Donna, caught somewhat unaware by this abrupt breaking of the silence, stammered slightly. "Why . . . ah . . . well, I imagine it is about as Uncle Jack said. Too much slackness and indifference due to the lack of competent authority. Sundown Sloan has done his best, but, as Uncle Jack said, he is old and he cannot stand the strain of hard riding any more.

"Some of the ranch hands have taken advantage of it. They've been soldiering on the job more or less. Uncle Jack tried firing a few of the worst, but those he hired in their place are just as bad. And then . . . well, we've missed more stock than is reasonable to expect from accidents, inclement weather, cougars, coyotes, and other things."

"You mean . . . rustlers?" demanded Buck crisply.

"Yes. You probably know what the Tonto Desert is . . . and the kind of men who ride it. They've grown bolder since age has slowed up Sundown. And you know how cowboys are about such things. Without a common leader they do lots of talking and riding without results."

"I see," muttered Buck. "And yet your uncle puts a proviso on this job that I don't pull a gun. Wonder how else he expects me to handle cattle rustlers? I reckon that's one place him and me ain't gonna agree. There's just one cure for rustlers . . . hot lead or a rope. Should the necessity arise, I reckon I'll use my own judgment and take a chance on what he'll say about it."

"I don't believe he was referring to rustlers when he asked that of you," defended Donna spiritedly. "Uncle Jack is no fool. He knows, as well as anyone else that certain malignant sicknesses require equally malignant remedies.

He was referring to the handling of the ranch within itself."

"I savvy," Buck said drily. "Who are your nearest neighbors?"

"Why the S C Connected adjoins our range on the east. Our ranch and theirs occupy practically all of Red Mesa."

"Who owns the S C Connected?"

"Slonicker and Canole."

Buck straightened in the saddle, his nostrils twitching. The color in his icy eyes deepened.

Donna, looking straight ahead, did not notice this momentary change in his attitude.

"Them two couldn't by any chance be Wolf Slonicker and Monk Canole?"

Startled at the sudden harshness of his voice, Donna darted a swift glance at him. But Buck's head was lowered as he licked a cigarette into shape.

"Why . . . yes, that is what they are called. Why? Have you known them before?"

"Yeah, I've knowed 'em before. They got a jasper named Curly Whipple ridin' for 'em?"

The dark blood flooded Donna's throat and face. She couldn't help it. She and Curly Whipple were very good friends—very good indeed.

"Yes," she murmured. "Curly is their foreman. Do you know him also?"

"I know him."

The words were so flat and cold, Donna flared.

"He's a nice boy . . . a good friend of mine."

"Oh sure," came the answering drawl, almost sardonic. "He would be. Yeah, he would be."

Donna's anger was swift. She had never met such a man as this. It seemed that every inflection, every tone of his voice carried some hidden meaning. And Buck's last words concerning Curly Whipple had fairly dripped contempt.

"See here, Mister Buck English," she stormed. "I don't like your tone a bit. I've long heard of you, of your self-centered, cold-blooded contempt for every creed, every law, every tenet of good citizenship. So, no matter what my uncle may see fit to do with you, don't presume to any scorn for my friends. Frankly, I fail to see that you are in any position to throw slurs . . . either spoken out or suggested . . . about anyone. You should sweep the dust from your own house before you notice that in someone else's."

Buck shrugged, saying nothing—but his eyes, as they fixed steadily on the trail ahead, grew colder and colder.

II

The buildings of the Red Mesa Ranch stood a scant quarter mile back from the mesa rim, overlooking the Tonto Desert. Here the higher crown of the mesa began to rise, fringed and matted with piñon, juniper, and mountain pine. Still farther back the timber thickened and spread, forming the watershed that fed the two great springs which supplied water to the ranch. These springs had been originally named by the Navajos, and, when Jack Carleton had first managed to translate the soft, musical gutturals of the natives, the north spring became the Silver Spring, the south, the Gold Spring.

There was no difference in the water. It was soft, crystal clear—cold and sweet. But the basins of rock from which burbled those precious, life-giving contents, were colored so that the similes were apt ones.

The ranch buildings were of the Spanish type, low and spreading, with thick walls, deep casements, and flat roofs. Freshly calcimined, they shone in the clear air and sunshine like monuments of white marble. The main ranch house was built about a square patio, rioting with colorful flowers, cheery with the song of birds, and a whisper with the murmur of running water brought by a tiny stone flume from the Silver Spring.

The corrals and feed sheds and other buildings stood farther east, skirting a wide basin that fed out onto the vast reaches of the mesa.

When Donna Carleton and Buck English finally reached headquarters, Donna lingered only long enough to introduce Buck to Sundown Sloan, with the announcement that her uncle had hired Buck as the new foreman, then went into the house, without a backward look or word.

Sundown Sloan was as grizzled as a badger, a stooped, crooked-legged old fellow, hunched with hardship, toil, and rheumatism. His face was colored and wrinkled until it resembled nothing so much as a piece of bark on a very old tree. But that there was nothing wrong with Sundown's mental faculties showed in the deep, sharp gleam of his eyes, set far back beneath shaggy brows.

There was satisfaction in those eyes as Sundown shook hands with Buck.

"Sho'," he drawled simply, "I'm powerful glad the boss picked you for this job, son, and I'm glad to know you. I knew your daddy well. You're a lot like him, when he was your age. His friendship is one of my best memories."

The quiet honesty of Sundown's words warmed Buck. For a moment the hardness, the stern chill of his face fled before a boyish smile. And his cold eyes softened.

"I'm always glad to meet one of dad's ole friends, Sundown. Sure, I hope you won't be takin' it to heart because Carleton's hired me for your old job."

"Me!" ejaculated Sundown. "Me sore. Shucks, boy . . . I'm tickled to death. I admit it kinda made me sour for a time to realize that age was gettin' me to a point where I couldn't handle the hard nuts of the crew any more. But common sense stomped that outta me. Every dawg has his day . . . and, Lord knows, I've had mine . . . and I'm makin' it plain that I'm mighty relieved to shift the worries and troubles of this cussed ranch to young shoulders again.

"I don't know whether Jack mentioned it to you . . . but it was my own suggestion that he get hold of somebody like you to take my place. I'm perfectly willin' to set back and let you handle things. And anything I can tell you or help you with, I'll be plumb tickled to do."

"That's mighty white of you, Sundown," Buck said. "While I'm puttin' my horse and Miss Donna's away . . . suppose you kinda give me a little drift of what I'm up against and what needs doin'."

As they walked down to the corrals, leading the two broncos, Sundown gnawed off a fresh chew of tobacco and squinted his eyes thoughtfully.

"First," he began, "you got a couple of fresh, wise jaspers to knock the corners off of. Buzz Layton and Pete Vanalia are the gents I mean. I cain't exactly figger them two fellers. I don't know whether we oughta fire 'em and be done with it . . . or whether a danged good lickin' will put 'em in the traces where they belong.

"They're both darned good hands . . . when they wanna hit the ball. But they're troublemakers and the kind that'll take advantage of you if they get a chance. Red Scudder is another hard nut. Independent as a hawg on ice. A good worker, but plumb set on doin' things his own way. And I'll tell you, he's a regular fire-eater in a scrap. Besides them three . . . we got Jiggs Maloney, Spud Enlow, Swede Sorenson, Dude McCollum, and Shorty Razee. They're all fine boys. Do their work, do it right, and never any trouble with 'em a-tall."

"I get you." Buck nodded, taking in the ranch yard. "But Jack Carleton didn't hire me just to comb the tails of a couple or three obstreperous 'punchers. There must be more to the story."

Sundown drenched a pop-eyed lizard with a stream of tobacco juice before answering.

"I'll tell the world there's more," he said portentously. "Handlin' the crew will be the least of your troubles. The big fly in the soup is that we're losin' stock altogether too regular to make this ranch a payin' proposition. Near as I can figger we lost nigh a hundred head last month alone.

"And then some ring-nosed polecat poisoned the Gold Spring last week. We use the water from the Gold Spring for the cattle. Bring it down in a ditch to those troughs you see out yonder. Well, before we found out what was wrong, we lost about sixty head of our Bar C beef and horses. I've had Shorty and Jiggs workin' all week on the spring, bailin' it out a dozen times or so. The water is just about fit to drink again now. Last fall we lost three stacks of winter feed we'd cut and piled. Somebody touched a match to 'em. Those are the sort of things that's gonna put gray hairs in your head, son."

Buck hung his saddle over the top rail of the corral and rolled a cigarette. "These cattle you been losin' . . . the rustled ones I mean . . . ain't there been any sign of how or where they went? Beef stock just don't grow wings and fly, you know, Sundown."

"No," admitted the old fellow, "they don't. I got a couple of ideas. But I don't know whether they're right or not. For one thing, there must be at least twenty or thirty different trails that the stock can get down off the mesa range to the desert. There's nothin' down there to attract them, Lord knows . . . but there's always some danged fool critters that are bound to wander. Once they get down there, they don't last long.

"No doubt the Navajos get a few of 'em for meat. But there's some mighty tough gangs of white renegades that ride that desert and they'd steal the pennies off a dead man's eyes. It grades up as an impossibility to keep enough riders on the move to watch the heads of all them trails, and the mesa rim is cut up so you can't fence 'em off without runnin' a fence around the whole rim. An it'd take a powerful lot of money to build such a fence. I tell you, Buck . . . it's a tough nut to crack."

"Seems so," agreed Buck. "Where does the S C Connected range run?"

Sundown darted a keen, questioning glance, but Buck's face was impassive and unreadable.

"Over yonder"—he pointed over his shoulder—"past the main crest of the mesa. They come in here after Jack did and had to take what was left. They got a lot of range over there, but it ain't worth a great deal. We catch most of the moisture here on the west side and the timber up above is heavy enough to hold it.

"On the S C Connected side the timber is pretty wide open and scarce. They ain't got any too much water, either. Two or three dry years back, they hadda cut their herds just about in half and then they hadda drive 'em down into Kanab Basin over past the east rim of the mesa. They sure don't make any money doin' that."

Buck pinched out his cigarette butt. "Good neighbors, are they?"

Again Sundown flashed that questioning glance at the young foreman. "Hmmm," he murmured. "I see you got ideas, Buck . . . same as me. Understand, I ain't hintin' or sayin' a thing. I couldn't prove nothin' if I did say it. Long ago I learned that it paid a feller to keep his mouth shut unless he had somethin' worthwhile to talk about. Just the same . . ."

He stopped mid-sentence, ended it with a shrug.

Buck smiled slightly, the old, cold glitter in his eyes. He took a new tack.

"I can't savvy why Jack Carleton don't work his authority in his own interests more, Sundown."

Sundown grunted and spat in huge disgust. He studied the mesa for several minutes before responding.

"Wouldn't he like to. But that's what he gets for dabblin' around in politics. The opposition that run ag'in' Jack last election time are sore as all get-out over bein' licked. They watch him like a hawk. Was he to spend any time out here tryin' to straighten out his own troubles, they'd be on his neck like a swarm of ants.

"He tried it once and they like to remove him on the charge of usin' the authority of his office to serve his own ends. It was a lie of course, but they made it stick with a lot of folks. So, instead of turnin' him loose to knock the corners off in a rustler or two, they keep him tied to his office, servin' summons for this and that, and a lot of other petty larceny stuff. They'll work hell outta him to help everybody but hisself. There they seem to draw a line."

"Who was the opposition at the last election?"

"Curt Daggett. He's a big man around Cedarville. Got his fingers in all kinds of pie. Owns a couple of stores, the hotel, a saloon, and is even a director of the bank. If he'd got the job of sheriffin' he'd just about owned the whole danged county before he got put out, I reckon. Well, c'mon over to the bunkhouse and store your war bag. I understand that when Jack got in touch with you, you were clear over past the Madrigals. You musta had quite some ride. You look a little fagged. Before you start lookin' around, you better get some rest."

Sunset, from the west rim of Red Mesa, was a sight few were fortunate enough to see. No painting could begin to portray the stupendous beauty of the thing. The Tonto Desert below, turning from a red, hostile gulf to a dreamy sea of indescribable mauves and violets and purples. The blazing streamers of sun-tinted clouds that poured out of the west, the glittering fire of the Madrigal Peaks, leagues out against that sunset sky, wild, aloof, haunting, lonely. And then the swift fading light, which left the Madrigals stark and cold while the desert grew black and deep and veiled.

Seldom indeed did Donna Carleton miss watching the sight of the sunset. It was her habit to walk to the rim, seat herself on a favorite rock, and give free rein to fancy and romance. Somehow she came back rested, humble, grateful—soothed to a quiet gentleness, no matter how strenuous the day had been.

But this evening she did not go down to her

favorite seat. She had started, but she got just far enough to see that the seat had been usurped. A man was down there, a rider—with flat, straight shoulders and a high, proud cast to his head. She then knew it was Buck English.

At first Donna's chin had come up defiantly. Why shouldn't she go down if she liked? What difference if he was there? Yet, restraint and that same shyness gripped her. She grew angry—with him as well as herself. He was an interloper, intruding on her privacy of dreams and visions. He should be put in his place. But, even as she thought of this, Donna knew that her courage was not equal to the task.

Something about the man made her uneasy, made her as self-conscious and shy as a child, and she felt helpless to combat his influence.

But as she withdrew to the house in piqued silence, she had to admit that he fitted the picture perfectly. He was a part of that same wild land, his eyes keen with the reading of those same illimitable distances. And the chill of the encroaching night was reflected in him. Also, thought Donna, he was as deep and inscrutable as the desert—as cold and unapproachable as the distant Madrigals.

III

Buck was introduced to the crew over the evening meal in the grub shack. At Buck's previous request, Sundown had not included the information that the foremanship of the ranch had changed hands. Buck had decided that could wait until they were all gathered in the privacy of the bunkhouse, later in the evening. For, if there were to be any objections to the new boss, Buck wanted to argue them out there, not in the grub shack where there were dishes and other equipment to break.

Buck knew that he was the object of a somewhat furtive scrutiny by most of the ranch hands, and he used the opportunity of the meal to make his own estimate of the others. He soon decided that Sundown Sloan had judged the cowpunchers pretty closely to right.

Red Scudder was the strongest personality of the lot. He was a big, gaunt, raw-boned fellow with a stubborn, fighting jaw, cold blue eyes, and a flaming shock of hair. Handled right, Scudder would be a friend worthwhile.

Buzz Layton and Pete Vanalia were of a type common in the frontier towns Buck had known west of the Madrigals. Rough, hard-faced, calculating, with capabilities for waywardness greater than those of industry and faithfulness to their trust.

The rest were pretty much everyday cow-punchers, reacting readily to the right kind of leadership. Jiggs Maloney was a comical little Irishman, and he and Shorty Razee, the youngest of all of them, were the clowns of the outfit.

Buck did not go immediately to the bunkhouse. Instead he smoked a cigarette and wandered thoughtfully around the patio of the ranch house, where the night air was heavy and fragrant with the incense of the flowers.

His thoughts turned to Donna Carleton. He smiled a little bitterly. Funny how women disliked him. He did not know why. But they did—and Donna Carleton was no exception. Was it his reputation, built up unreasonably by lesser men, careless with their tongues? Perhaps that had something to do with it.

On his part, Buck had always admired the right sort of women. His tongue had never been facile enough to tell any of them so, however. Because of this inability to say the right thing in the right way to any of them, coupled with their own immediate aversion for him, Buck had passed them all by, leaving the conquest of them to luckier—or unluckier men—than himself. Not that there was no romance in him—no hunger for the realities of life. There was—plenty of it.

But the shyness that he felt did not show and the hard, masterful, almost callous mask he had built about himself seemed to awaken a strange resentment in the opposite sex. It was as though they realized immediately that here was a man who they could never master, never gentle, influence, or control.

There was a stone seat in one corner of the patio, where the shadows were deep, and here Buck rested, aloof and lonely. He crumpled the butt of his cigarette and rolled another. But he did not light it, for a nearby door had opened.

He saw Donna Carleton standing there, etched against the light within like a slender shadow. She stepped out into the patio, closing the door behind her. Instantly she caught the lingering tang of tobacco smoke from Buck's dead cigarette. She looked about alertly.

"Curly!" she called softly. "You here already?"

Buck stirred. "Sorry," he drawled. "This is English. I didn't mean to intrude. But I like flowers. I hoped you wouldn't mind if I hung around a bit. But as you're expectin' company . . . I'll drift along."

Donna was startled and a little angry. Startled because she was somehow afraid of Buck English; angry because she had carelessly announced the fact that she was expecting a visit from Curly Whipple, for whom Buck English had previously shown he held nothing but a sardonic contempt. For a moment her temper was close to the surface. Then her common sense took command.

"Of course," she announced lightly. "There is no reason why you should apologize for your presence. As foreman, the run of the ranch is yours. It is I who am intruding."

She turned as though to go back into the house, but Buck forestalled her.

He spoke words that were as startling to him as they were to Donna.

"Don't go. Can't we be a little more friendly? You don't seem to have much use for me, but we're bound to have to see considerable of one another here at the ranch, and there ain't any sense in us sidlin' around each other like a pair of strange bulldogs. There's plenty of room on this bench for the two of us."

Donna laughed as she seated herself.

"You astound me, Mister English. I can't conceive of you being interested in the company of a woman . . . not after what I've heard. I'm afraid this rather shows you up as a faker. Your self-sufficiency isn't altogether satisfactory, is it? You know what loneliness is, after all."

"I reckon," he said gravely. "Yeah . . . I know what loneliness is. No man knows it better than I do. When your uncle offered me this job it kind of opened a new view on life to me. I wanna make it stick. The lone wolf travels fast and far

. . . but he never knows the comforts of a den. Maybe you won't believe it . . . but I'm human."

She began to see him in a new light. Somehow he seemed wistful—almost pathetic in his isolation. Her tone changed.

"I like you so much better . . . this way," she said quietly.

Instantly she was panicky. Those words had slipped out before she knew it.

"Thanks," he said, a trifle huskily. "You've no idea how much that means to me. You see . . . women have always shied off around me. Seems like they felt I was sort of an animal . . . a dangerous beast . . . a killin' machine or some fool thing. That's always hurt me some, though, before now, I've never admitted it. Not that I was particularly interested in women. I wasn't. But it got me to feelin' that maybe they were right. And that certainly didn't help my constitution any. If you'll just keep on bein' friendly to me . . . it'll sure help a lot."

Donna tried to laugh lightly, but the laugh was just a little shaky. For of a sudden she realized that this cold-faced young cowpuncher was a strange and powerful personality. There was an arresting beauty about him, a beauty of soul, rather than of flesh. He had lived apart from the pack, trod his own trails, followed his own visions. Men might hate him—but she understood they could not help respecting him. They might hate him because they feared him, but they saluted him for his indomitable courage, his unflinching power of purpose, his deadliness in conflict. And yet, despite this, there was a boyish wistfulness about him—a timid, shy hunger for the warmth of friendship.

"I am wondering . . . ," Donna started to say softly, but then she hesitated when she realized she was starting to tremble. Finally she decided to blurt it out. "I am wondering if you have ever spoken this way to anyone else. I don't believe you ever have."

"No," he answered, taken aback by his ability to talk so openly with her. "I never have."

"Then I am particularly honored. And I shall respect your confidence. Also, we shall be friends . . . Buck."

She sensed him start, at her use of his name.

He stood up, lean and tall. "I'll be driftin' now," he said. "I wanna hang on to this . . . before somethin' happens to spoil it."

At that moment came the sound of thudding hoofs, approaching through the night. They came close, changed to a trot, then ceased altogether. Spur chains clashed softly and the figure of a rider stepped into the patio.

It was Curly Whipple.

"I should've left before," Buck said softly, in a voice that had gone flat and repressed again. "This sure does spoil everythin'."

Donna caught his arm. "What do you mean by that?" she demanded.

He laughed harshly. "You wouldn't believe me, anyway. And the fool ethics of man keep him from talkin' about some things."

He tried to pull away, but Donna would not let go. Angry perversity gripped her.

She called out: "Curly! Here I am . . . over at the bench. I want you to meet a friend of mine."

Whipple crossed to them, a lean, smoothly moving bulk in the darkness. "Sorry I was late, Donna," he explained.

"But I met Buzz and Pete headin' for town and I stopped to chew the rag with 'em for a while. Oh-h!" His voice hardened slightly. "It's a gentleman friend, is it?"

"Yes," said Donna sharply. "Meet Buck English, Curly."

Whipple was like a man thunderstruck. He stopped dead in his tracks, his shoulders hunched, his hands dangling suggestively.

Buck laughed. "Careful, Whipple," he drawled icily. "There's a lady present. and I left my guns down in the bunkhouse. I reckon I oughta say I'm pleased to meet you. But I won't . . . 'cause I'm not. Besides, we've met before . . . haven't we, Whipple? A long time back."

For a moment Whipple was inarticulate. Then his words came harshly. "Buck English! What you doin' here?"

"If it'll interest you . . . and it probably will . . . you as well as Slonicker and Canole. I'm the new foreman of this spread. Miss Donna and me have just been admirin' the night and the smell of the flowers. But three's a crowd. And seein' that you and Miss Donna got a previous date, I'll amble along."

This time Donna could not keep her grasp on his arm. His free hand settled upon her wrist like a band of flexible steel, lifting her grip free, gentle yet inexorable. Then he was gone.

To Donna Carleton it seemed as though the night had turned cold. The velvety gloom of the patio was oppressive, threatening. For the stark, abysmal hate that flashed between these two men had held the breath of death about it somehow.

Whipple was still hunched, staring at the spot where Buck had disappeared. His breath came gustily—between set, snarling teeth. He was muttering something, scalding curses it sounded like to Donna.

"How long has that *hombre* been around this ranch?" he demanded harshly.

Donna moved a little apart from him, her chin up.

"I don't care for your tone, Curly Whipple," she declared crisply. "Unless you can change it . . . I'll say good night."

Whipple put forth a detaining hand.

"Wait," he blurted. "Sorry, Donna. I beg your pardon. But him . . . Buck English . . . seein' him here kind of upset me."

"Why should it?"

Whipple drew a deep breath. "It startles you, don't it . . . when you run face to face with a rattler? If you reach out your hand to shake with someone and find out that that someone is a rabid coyote, you're bound to be surprised, ain't you? And he says he's the new foreman here. That can't be so, Donna."

"But it is so," she answered stiffly. "Uncle Jack hired him today. And I'm afraid I don't agree with you, Curly Whipple. He doesn't strike me as being anything poisonous or unclean. He's different, yes . . . vastly different than any man I've ever met. How do you know he is what you claim? Where have you known him before?"

The darkness hid the film of wariness that veiled Whipple's eyes.

"I knew him over past the Madrigals. The men over there, that truly know him, would cut their own throats before they'd put him in charge of their ranch. Gawd! Your Uncle Jack must be crazy."

Despite herself, Donna knew a vague doubt of Buck English. Certainly Whipple's words and tone seemed sincere enough—and convincing. And only a great hate, or great fear or feeling of utter repulsion could have affected Whipple as the meeting had. In all fairness Donna considered the fact that she had known Curly Whipple a great deal longer than she had known Buck English. And Curly had always seemed nice enough— likable, happy-go-lucky, and considerate.

On the other hand, Buck English was cold, reserved, deep, and unreadable. From others she had heard hints of his reputation, his ferocity, his ability and will to kill. Perhaps his attitude as they had talked there in the patio was nothing more than a pose after all. Yet, there had been wistfulness. . . .

More in defense of her uncle's judgment than anything else, Donna held her ground.

"I find it hard to truly believe all that, Curly," she said. "Uncle Jack is nobody's fool. *He* has faith and trust in Buck English."

Whipple shrugged in restless anger. "All men make mistakes. It won't be long before you find that your uncle has made a big one. Well . . . I've got to be driftin'. I just dropped in for a hello. I'll be seein' you. ¡*Adiós*!"

Donna did not try and hold him. The abruptness of his leaving was not at all in accord with his usual habit. It was all quite obvious that the presence of Buck English in a position of authority at the Red Mesa Ranch had a disturbing effect on Curly Whipple, which had driven all thought of romance from his mind.

He was either very much afraid, or the news

was of such importance that he was in a wild hurry to broadcast it. In either event, Donna knew that she could never look upon Curly Whipple in the same light of friendship she had previously held for him.

IV

Buzz Layton and Pete Vanalia did not arrive back from town until nearly noon of the following day. Their faces clearly showed that they had put in a wild night of drinking. Their eyes were bloodshot, their features bloated.

Buck English was down at the cavvy corral when they rode up. As they dismounted he sauntered over to them. Neither Layton nor Vanalia paid any attention to him. But Buck thrust his way before them, building a deft cigarette.

"Kind of late gettin' back on the job, ain't you, boys?" he drawled quietly.

Layton grunted, but Vanalia cursed savagely. "Who the hell wants to know?"

"I do," snapped Buck, the chill in his eyes deepening. "I'm runnin' this spread now. And I'm here to tell you that if you want to keep on ridin' for this layout, you're gonna hit the ball and earn your wages. After quittin' time on Saturday nights, up until work time starts Monday mornin' . . . your time is your own. But Jack Carleton ain't

133

payin' you wages to go on sprees in the middle of the week. Don't let it happen again. I'm tellin' you somethin'."

"Is that so?" sneered Vanalia. "Well, let me tell you somethin', feller. Over past the Madrigals you mighta been hell a-wheelin'. But here you're just a wise young jasper tryin' to show some new authority. So I'm announcin' it don't get by a bit with Buzz and me."

Buck smiled grimly. "You feel the same way about it, Layton?"

"Yeah," growled Buzz. "I feel the same way about it."

"*Bueno*. You're both fired. Pack your war bags and hit the trail. I'll give you a note on your time. Take it to Jack Carleton and he'll pay you off. That's all."

The two recalcitrants were honestly amazed. They had had their own way about the ranch for so long that this new order of things rather knocked their feet from under them for a moment.

But their astonishment was only momentary. Vanalia cursed again and went on unsaddling. Layton followed suit.

"It'll take a better man than you to fire us," rasped Vanalia. "Don't push us too far or we'll knock the kinks outta you."

Buck shrugged, inhaled deeply, and tossed his cigarette aside. Then he went into action like a tiger on the kill. Layton was the closest and Buck

134

knocked him flat with the first punch. He went right on over Layton's falling body, catapulting into the squat, powerful Vanalia with both fists pumping.

Vanalia drew his gun, but Buck was too close to him. His gun hand was knocked aside and a terrific, lifting blow caught the ranch hand squarely under the heart. Vanalia gasped and sagged, his knees bending. A flailing fist crashed home to his face, driving him still farther back—half blinding him. He tried to get some distance between himself and this human catapult—distance to swing his own powerful fists. But he never had a chance to get set. That thudding tattoo of driving punches never stopped for a second. He began to flounder unsteadily. A whistling right hook bounced off the angle of his sullen jaw and he went down, sliding through the dust on his shoulders.

A yell of warning sounded behind Buck. He whirled, just in time to see Buzz Layton lift himself on one elbow, steadying his gun for a center shot.

Buck did not have his guns on him and it looked bad. He tensed for a leap at Layton, but a big, red-headed thunderbolt beat him to it.

It was Red Scudder, who had run out of the saddle shed at the first sound of conflict. Now he was clear in the air, pouncing like a great cat. He slammed down on Layton just as the latter pulled the trigger. The bullet flicked the loose folds of Buck's neckerchief as it passed. But then a big, freckled fist rose and fell like a club, and Layton went limp once more.

Red secured Layton's gun and got to his feet. Buck was busy punching the cartridges from Vanalia's weapon. This done, he walked over to Red, his hand outstretched.

"Much obliged, Red," he said simply. "I owe you one for that."

Red shrugged and grinned, as their hands met. "That was a dirty trick Buzz tried," he drawled. "I couldn't let him get away with it. Besides, those two jaspers just got somethin' that's been comin' to 'em for a long time. They've been overdue for a lickin' for far too long."

Buck handed Vanalia's gun to Red. "Hang on to both those hog-legs until these jaspers are ready to leave. I'll go look over the books and see how much time they got comin'. If they get obstreperous, peel 'em again."

The foreman's office was a tiny, end room beside the opening into the patio.

Buck had just finished figuring out the time of the two cowpunchers, when Donna Carleton stepped through the door. She was a little pale— but defiant.

"I . . . I saw that fight," she announced. "Was it necessary?"

"I figured it was," answered Buck quietly. "I fired 'em and they sorta boiled over. I had to show 'em who was boss."

"But they had done nothing to be fired for."

"Sorry, Miss Donna . . . I see it different. They was soldierin' on your uncle. The other boys were all on the job, earnin' their wages. Layton and Vanalia weren't. If they'd acted reasonable when I reminded 'em of it, nothin' would have happened. But I called 'em and they wanted a fight. They got it."

"But you're making the ranch short-handed," argued Donna, realizing plainly that her arguments were useless, and furious because of it.

"I can get some more to take their places," Buck said. He stood up and reached for his hat. "I'm sorry you don't like the way I'm goin' about things. But I was sent out here to run this ranch . . . and I'm gonna run it."

His teeth clicked over this last statement and Donna could not meet the level power of his eyes. She turned and went out of the room.

Buck went down to the bunkhouse.

Layton and Vanalia were ready to leave. Buck handed over their time slips.

Red Scudder was lounging in the door of the bunkhouse, the cowpunchers' empty guns dangling in his hands. At a nod from Buck he gave them to their owners.

Pete Vanalia holstered his weapon and swung

into the saddle. Then he stared down at Buck with flat, deadly eyes.

"This thing ain't finished, English," he said thickly through swollen lips. "Our turn will come . . . one of these days."

Buck shrugged. "Life works out that way sometimes, Vanalia. But I'll remember you promised it."

Vanalia cursed and spurred away, Layton falling in beside him.

Red Scudder watched their disappearing figures with narrowed eyes. "I *would* remember, Buck . . . was I you," he murmured. "I'll say this for Pete Vanalia. He's got nerve . . . and a hell of a long memory. Layton's the weak sister of the two."

"I judged so," agreed Buck. "Well, looks like I got to ride to town this afternoon and pick up a couple or more hands. Think you could stand the exercise, Red?"

Red's blue eyes gleamed. "¡*Bueno*! I don't mind sayin' I like your style, Buck."

Their eyes met and locked.

Buck smiled slowly. "I reckon we understand each other, Red."

In the back room of the Silver King Saloon a conference was in session. Four men were present, seated around a scarred table on which rested a half-filled whiskey bottle and several glasses.

Curt Daggett, a tall man with narrow shoulders and a bulging, sagging waistline, was speaking. His pale, washed-out-looking eyes were gleaming with anger and perturbation and his thin lips scarcely moved as the bitter words dripped from them.

"No question about it . . . we've been working too slow and cautious," he declared. "Now the going will be slower and tougher than ever. It doesn't do any good for you to try and belittle Buck English to me, Curly. That jasper didn't get his fighting reputation on hot air and bluff.

"If you don't think he's a tiger . . . ask Buzz and Pete. I was just out front talking to 'em a few minutes ago, and Pete . . . though it hurts his feelings to admit it . . . says that English is all he's rated to be. On top of that, he's made a friend of Red Scudder . . . and Red rates a pretty tough *hombre* himself. So our job hasn't gotten any simpler, not by a damned sight. Question is . . . what do we do?"

Monk Canole blurted into speech. His nickname aptly described him. His physical make-up was strongly simian in type. His shoulders were sloped and stooping, with long, loose hanging arms. His legs were short and bowed. His nose was flat and spreading, his eyes little and round and set deep beneath beetling brows, above which his brow was low and sharply slanting.

"You shoulda listened to me a long time ago,

139

Daggett," he growled. "When you're gamblin' for high stakes, you gotta play your cards like you mean it. You cain't keep 'em close to your vest. We been follerin' your plan so far, and all we've done is put Carleton on his guard. He's imported the fightinest hellion I know of to run his ranch. And English knows Wolf and Curly and me. I tell you, we've made a mess of things. How about it, Wolf?"

"You're right, Monk," Wolf Slonicker said, taking in the rest of the men with his sharp eyes. "Buck English bein' on the job sure don't help our chances none. We shoulda struck out hard and heavy before this. Now, I dunno just what to do."

Slonicker was tall and thin and cadaverous, with long black hair, shallow eyes, and narrow, protruding features. At the moment he was chewing nervously on a splinter of wood he had whittled from the table edge.

"Seems like English has sure got you fellows buffaloed," Curly Whipple said, sneering. "To hear you jaspers talk you'd think he was a company of United States cavalry all by himself."

Canole cursed. "You always was a damned fool, Whipple. You can make a lot of big talk, but in a showdown you don't amount to much. If you had the brains of an ant, you wouldn't try to put that hogwash over about English bein' a soft-shelled *hombre*. In your heart you know better

. . . and you know you're scared stiff of him. You're jest whistlin' to keep from breakin' down into tears. Me, I'm honest enough to admit that I'd rather tackle a nest of bobcats than I would Buck English. I'd have more chance of comin' out alive. So unless you can talk sense, shut up!"

"Monk's talkin' gospel, Curt," said Slonicker to Daggett. "I tell you, English is a tiger."

Daggett, who had been drumming his fingers on the table, lifted his head in decision. "I'll take your word for it, boys. Which means . . . English has got to be removed . . . the quicker the better. Got any ideas?"

For a time there was no answer. Then Canole shifted restlessly.

"Dry-gulchin' is the best bet I know. It won't do to try and meet him face to face and call him out. Whoever tried it would be dead . . . *pronto* . . . and English would still be saunterin' along. But a Thirty-Thirty slug sifted into him from ambush ought to do the trick . . . providin' the fellow who tried it didn't miss. Besides, that way we can still cover our tracks. Jack Carleton won't be able to lay his finger on us."

"Sounds reasonable . . . and safe," Daggett said, nodding his approval. "And with English out of the way . . . we'll quit the petty larceny stuff and make some real moves. Who's a good rifle shot?"

Canole leered. "Whipple ain't so bad, and he

seems to think that knockin' off English wouldn't be much of a chore. Why not elect him?"

Curly Whipple paled. He was very passably good-looking until his eyes and mouth were studied. The eyes were pale blue and shifty. His mouth was pouty and weak. His sandy hair was attractively curly and there was a pink glow beneath the tan of his face. One's first impression of Curly Whipple was favorable—but knowing him as he really was could promptly change that.

"Why pick on me?" he protested. "I'm just a 'puncher, drawin' wages from the S C Connected spread. You three fellows got a lot more at stake than me. No, sir . . . I won't do it."

Monk Canole's beady eyes turned red. "I reckon, Whipple . . . concernin' everythin' I know . . . you will do it . . . if I say so."

Whipple licked his lips, started to say something but changed his mind and nodded. "Okay, Monk," he mumbled.

The first stop of Buck English and Red Scudder when they reached town was Sheriff Jack Carleton's office. By good luck they found Carleton in.

Buck came to the point immediately and briefly. "I gave Layton and Vanalia their time, Jack."

Carleton smiled tightly. "So I noticed, Buck.

They just left here. I gave 'em their checks. Little argument, wasn't there?"

"Yeah . . . some. They got hostile when I told 'em they were all done. Red and me come in to see if we could pick up a couple of riders to take their place. Got any idea where we might find any?"

Carleton nodded. "Yeah. I got a line on a couple already. Look like pretty fair hands to me. You'll find 'em at the hotel. Names are Evans and Drake. Go and look 'em over. They suit me, if they suit you. I had a hunch you'd have trouble with Layton and Vanalia. Anythin' else new out at the ranch?"

Buck rolled a cigarette carefully. He nodded. "What do you know about Slonicker, Canole, and Curly Whipple, Jack?"

Carleton was startled.

"Not a great deal. They're our closest neighbors to the ranch. But they mind their business and . . ."

"I wonder," broke in Buck crisply. "I wonder if they do mind their own business. How long they been here?"

"Lemme see. Somethin' like five years for Slonicker and Canole. Whipple came in more recent. Why?"

"Five years, eh? That checks up. They must've come straight here from Welkin Valley and down there past the Madrigals. Well, Jack . . . they left Welkin Valley with an open noose waitin' for 'em if they ever came back. Rumor had it that Whipple was connected with 'em, too. Sundown has been tellin' me about things, and before I worry much about the Tonto Desert men, I'm gonna look the S C Connected over pretty darned careful." Buck turned to face Scudder. "Red, it's gettin' late. Let's pick up those two riders and hit the trail. So long, Jack."

For some time after the two had left, Carleton sat in thought. Finally he shrugged and smiled grimly.

"I knew I wasn't makin' any mistake in gettin' hold of Buck," he muttered. "I knew Slonicker and Canole were off-color, but I sorta figured Whipple as bein' a fairly decent sort. I reckon I better tell Donna to have nothin' more to do with him. Buck seems pretty sure about all three of 'em."

At the hotel Buck located the two riders, Slim Evans and Chuck Drake. He approved the moment he saw them. They were young fellows, but capable-looking—and square shooters if Buck knew anything about human nature. Forty and found evidently met their approval, for they rounded up their horses and rode out with Buck and Red.

Dusk caught them halfway up the mesa trail. Buck was in the lead, with Red Scudder, Evans, and Drake following in the order named. Where the trail cut around the head of a narrow, brush-choked ravine which angled downward across the flank of the mesa, Buck pulled in to breathe his horse, advising the others to do the same.

He rolled a cigarette and scratched a match, turning sideways in the saddle to shield the flame from the rising push of the night wind. As he bent his head toward the light, a lance of crimson flame spurted from the ravine, a gun bellowed in report, and some mysterious force cut the cigarette clean from his lips. At the same instant a queer, crunching spat sounded behind Buck, and Red Scudder slid from his saddle like an empty sack.

V

Donna Carleton was drowsing in an armchair, trying to make up her mind whether or not to retire for the night, when she was roused by a sharp, peremptory knock on the door. Startled, and with a premonition of trouble gripping her, she crossed the room quickly and opened the portal.

The light, slanting over her shoulder, showed the cold, intent features of Buck English.

Donna did not miss the expression of his eyes.

"Some- . . . something has happened?" she stammered.

He nodded. "Yes. Red Scudder has been shot. A dry-gulcher cut down on us as we were climbing the mesa. He's not dead. But I need hot water and bandages. You've got an emergency kit here, Sundown tells me."

"Yes. I'll get it for you. And I'll have the cook rustle up some hot water immediately."

She ran out of the room, called some directions to Sevila, the Mexican cook, then came hurrying back with a first-aid kit. She handed it to Buck and drew on a light sweater.

"No need your comin' down to the bunkhouse," objected Buck. "I can fix Red up all right."

Donna's answer was to push by him. Buck shrugged and followed.

Red Scudder lay on a bunk, his eyes open, but full of pain. The rest of the cowpunchers stood about, quiet and serious. A dusty, blood-soaked neckerchief was bound around Red's head. He managed a twisted smile for Donna.

"Sho' now, Miss Donna," he whispered. "There ain't no need you botherin' about me. Ole Buck'll fix this head of mine."

Donna's face was a little pale, but she did not waver.

"No more talking, if you please, Red," she ordered. "Steady now . . . until I get this filthy bandage off."

Red was steady enough, but Donna herself was

the one who grew shaky as she saw the ragged, angry, blood-clotted tear where the bullet that had been intended for Buck had ripped its vicious way across the top of Red's head.

Buck gently but firmly pushed her aside.

"You can help," he said, not unkindly. "But leave the main job to me."

When the hot water arrived, Buck carefully shaved about the wound, cleansed it thoroughly, and drew it together with several rather expertly placed sutures. A clean, firm bandage in place and the job was finished.

"Now you roll over and go to sleep, you knot-headed old maverick," said Buck to Red. "You'll be feelin' a heap better by mornin'."

Red grinned through white lips. "Okay. Gimme another drink of *agua*."

The light was shaded and the rest of the ranch hands followed Buck outside.

Jiggs Maloney caught Buck by the arm. "Are ye after finishin' the job tonight, Buck?" he asked. "Begorra, me and the rest of the boys are sure itchin' to pull on a rope."

Buck shook his head. "No, Jiggs. I'm aimin' to make that jasper talk and find out who sicced him on us. I leave it up to you and the boys to see that he doesn't get away."

"Sure, and ye need waste no worry over that!" exploded Jiggs. " 'Tis meself who'll roost on the spalpeen's tail like a ghost after a scaredy cat.

Shorty and me'll be with him for the rest of the night."

As Buck started for his office, Donna fell into step with him.

"What Jiggs just said . . . does that mean you caught the one who did the shooting?" she asked him nervously.

"Yeah, we nailed him. Rode him down and pistol-whipped him. He's locked up in the saddle shed."

"Who . . . who was it?"

Buck hesitated. "I reckon you'd feel better if you didn't know," he drawled finally.

"Bosh! I insist on knowing. If you won't tell me . . . well, I'll ask one of the boys. Who is it?"

Buck shrugged. "If you insist . . . Curly Whipple."

Donna stopped stock still. She caught her breath in an unconscious gasp of protest.

"No . . . no! That can't be true. Curly . . . Curly would never do a thing like that. He isn't that sort. I tell you it's a mistake. You're wrong. I don't believe it!"

"You saw Red's head. There ain't no mistake. We caught Whipple cold."

"But why . . . why should Curly do such a thing?" she muttered as much to herself as to Buck.

"I reckon I could shoot pretty close to the

148

answer," Buck said grimly. "But I'm gonna let him tell it in his own words . . . tomorrow."

Donna had the feeling that she was beating futile fists against a cold, implacable stone wall. This fellow Buck English moved straight ahead, unheeding, remorseless, heartless—or so it seemed to the girl.

"He'll never admit to something he never did," she flamed.

A sardonic smile twisted Buck's lips. "Faith like you have is worthy of a better object, Miss Donna," he told her. "But he'll talk, never fear. There's a lot of ways of makin' a polecat like him open up."

"For shame! You speak like you were going to torture him . . . or . . . or something. You wouldn't dare."

"Wrong," was the level statement. "I'd dare anythin'. That jasper tried to dry-gulch me. He missed . . . but he came close to killin' Red Scudder . . . one of the first real friends I've made here on the ranch. Red saved me from bein' shot in the back by Buzz Layton. Anybody who hurts Red Scudder from here on out . . . hurts me. And I don't take kindly to bein' hurt . . . not even by you. Now you better run along to bed . . . and forget Curly Whipple. He ain't now . . . and he never was . . . worth one second of worry by you. Good night."

The door of his office closed behind him.

. . .

Donna felt almost as though he had slapped her in the face. Until now, she had always considered herself as somewhat of an authority about the ranch. Sundown Sloan had always made it a point to talk over any major problem with her. But this . . . this . . . Donna gritted her white teeth in a rising rage.

Buck English ignored her entirely, as far as her opinions went. Thrust her aside as though she were a child—suggested that she run along to bed.

She went to her room, but not to sleep. That was out of the question just now. Her thoughts were chaotic, her emotions upset.

For a time she paced to and fro in the confines of her bedroom, stifling her anger. After a bit she quieted and curled up in a chair to think.

Curly Whipple locked up—charged with attempted murder! It was a nightmarish thought.

Donna looked back. She had known Curly Whipple for a little more than a year. She sincerely liked him. She knew that her feelings toward Curly had never gone any deeper than this. But she *had* liked him. They had been good friends—nothing more. Her Uncle Jack had never objected to Curly's visiting with her. And surely—had Curly been off-color, as sheriff, her uncle would have known it.

On one occasion Curly had grown sentimental,

but Donna had checked his advances bruskly and it had never happened again. They had ridden together many times, and on one occasion she had gone to a dance in Cedarville with him. He had always been attentive, decent, and considerate. Now he was charged with an attempt at dastardly, cowardly murder. Donna could not bring herself to believe it.

On the other hand, there was no refuting the evidence of Red Scudder's wounded head. Someone had certainly fired the shot that did that. And Curly had apparently been caught in the act. But why? Why should he have attempted such a thing?

Then Donna thought of the meeting of Curly with Buck English in the patio the previous night. She remembered the cold undercurrent of hostility between them. And at that time Curly had seemed strange—foreign to her. She remembered his muttered curses, his scalding denunciation of English to her. Obviously there was hate between these two—hate fomented through previous meetings at some time in the past.

She remembered the short talk between English and herself before Curly had ridden up. At this, she felt a warm, subtle chill. Somehow she knew that she was the first of her sex who had ever glimpsed beyond that chill, abrupt curtain which shrouded the real personality of Buck English.

And she was just feminine enough to glory in this knowledge.

A new thought struck her. Why had English said what he had at the arrival of Curly—something to the effect of everything being spoiled now? There could be but one answer. It wasn't the fact that Curly had shown up to break the spell.

It was as though English felt a certain censure for her at her friendship with Whipple. As though it was besmirching—unworthy. And Buck had also added the statement, not fifteen minutes before, that Curly was not worthy of a thought or a moment of worry from her.

On the other hand, English was certainly in no position to criticize others. As a whole, his reputation was far more widespread and notorious than that of Curly. For until English had spoken, she had never heard a word against Curly.

True, Buck English's reputation was not an unmoral one. It was not mean, unclean, or unsavory. It had only to do with ruthlessness, cold unswerving fighting ability. It was that of an outlaw wolf, traveling a lone trail. Defiant, bold, careless of the conventions of law.

That he possessed fundamental requisites of stark manhood there could be no denying. But he was outspoken and brooked no interference with his authority. He was a man who a woman might follow, but never drive or master.

In summing up, Donna determined to hear the other side of the situation. She would have a talk with Curly.

It was nearly midnight when Donna stole from the house, edged through the patio, and went down toward the corrals. She had heard Jiggs Maloney assure Buck that he and Shorty would stand guard over the prisoner for the night and she was certain of her ability to sway the two cowpunchers. She preferred not to ask permission of Buck. She resented his authority for reasons of her own.

Jiggs and Shorty were wide awake and on the job. Jiggs's drawling brogue challenged Donna while she was still yards away from the saddle shed.

" 'Tis late ye are up this evening, Miss Donna," he said, coming to meet her. "And what'll ye be after losing your beauty sleep over?"

Donna knew it was useless to equivocate. "Jiggs, I want to have a talk with Curly Whipple. I can't help but feel that there is some mistake somewhere. I've known Curly a long time. I just can't believe he did this. And I want to hear from him his side of the story."

Jiggs shuffled his feet uneasily.

"Sure . . . and 'tis wasted sympathy, Miss Donna," he mumbled. " 'Tis a crooked, murdering, cowardly snake that Whipple is. Badness is in him, say I. Had I my way . . . he would've been kicking air, hanging from a rope hours ago. Now be a sensible girl and just go on back to the house and leave him to Shorty and me. I don't think Buck would be after liking ye talking to him."

"That's neither here nor there, Jiggs," replied Donna sharply. "Mister English may be foreman of this ranch, but his authority does not extend over me and my actions. I do not intend to aid Curly in escape. I merely want to talk to him. Surely there can be no harm in that," she said, pausing before adding: "I demand that you let me see him."

Jiggs fumbled for a reply. He wished silently that Buck would show up on scene and take over the responsibility of agreeing with or denying Donna's wish. He stepped back, scratching his head.

"Are . . . are ye sure ye aren't after helping him get away?" he said, wavering about his orders.

"For shame," retorted Donna. "Of course I'm not. I have no weapon to give him or anything of the sort. I merely feel that he is entitled to tell his own story to someone who is not too prejudiced against him. Come, Jiggs . . . unlock the door for me."

Jiggs swore softly and led the way to the door of the saddle shed, where Shorty rose from the steps at sight of the two.

"Miss Donna here wants to talk to that spalpeen inside, Shorty," Jiggs growled to Shorty's wondering exclamation of surprise. "See that ye watch the door careful while I open it."

Jiggs pounded lustily on the portal. "Ye . . . Whipple. Are ye awake?"

"Yeah . . . I'm awake. What do you want?"

"Me?" Jiggs snapped, and paused before continuing. "I want to see ye kicking in a noose. But 'tis Miss Donna who wishes to talk to you. I'm opening the door, but should ye make one phony move, I will plug ye like I would a polecat."

Jiggs waited briefly before turning the key. Then he drew his gun and kicked the door open.

He kept his eyes on the doorway of the shed when addressing Donna. "In ye go, Miss Donna. When ye are done . . . holler."

Donna entered the murky interior, waiting for her eyes to adjust to the dark.

"Curly," she said softly. "I want you to tell me your story of what happened."

The door closed behind her. The interior of the place was shrouded with murk. She could not see her hand before her face. Suddenly an inexplicable fear gripped her. She stepped back until her shoulders struck the door.

"Curly!" she called again. "Haven't you anything to say?"

A surly growl answered from the other end of

the room. "What's the use of me sayin' anything? You won't believe me."

"You don't know whether I will or not. Surely you must realize that I wouldn't come here like this if I was absolutely convinced of your guilt. I felt that you were entitled to a hearing by someone who would be fair. Of course . . . if you feel differently . . . I'll go."

"There ain't a heap to tell," answered Whipple, his tone still harsh.

Donna heard the scrape of a foot, which made her jump. She was glad it was too dark for Curly to see her clearly.

"I was ridin' the trail to town and was droppin' down the mesa side. Just as I hit a turn in the trail a shot sounded in a gulch below me. The next thing I knew a bunch of riders came surgin' up. Naturally I spun my horse and tried to make a ride of it. It was just about dark and I couldn't recognize any of 'em. For all I knew that shot might've been aimed at me. Anyhow, I did some spurrin'.

"But somebody had a faster horse than me. They caught me in about ten jumps and pistol-whipped me. That was all I knew until I woke up in this shed. That buzzard, Buck English, was here . . . and when I told him what I told you, he gave me that horse laugh. Damn his arrogant, cold-blooded soul! All I ask is to get one more . . . I mean a chance at him . . . and I'll

156

sift lead into him if it's the last thing I ever do."

Donna had been listening too closely to miss the slip that Whipple made. He had started to say— "get one more chance at him." Of that Donna was certain. And it meant that Whipple was lying— that he *had* been the one that had fired the shot at Buck but had creased Red Scudder instead.

She sighed wearily. "I've heard enough. You're lying. I've never been more certain."

She turned toward the door, her lips parted to call to Jiggs.

And then there sounded a creak of boards, a slithering footstep. Before she could move, hard, clawing hands struck her shoulders, shifted quickly to her throat. But her call was already framed and sounded before that sudden cruel stricture could halt it.

"Jiggs!"

The door creaked open and Donna, choking and struggling blindly, was hurled through it. She smashed into Jiggs and fell away and the ground rose to meet her with a crash. She had a hazy impression of a crouching bulk lunging past her, heard the impact of a hard-swung fist—a single shot—then darkness, deep and unfathomable.

VI

The bite of raw whiskey in her throat brought Donna back to consciousness. She choked and gagged over the stimulant, for her throat felt tight and raw. Her head ached abominably.

She opened her eyes dazedly, to find a circle of anxious faces peering down at her. Foremost among them were the inscrutable features of Buck English. Beside him was the round, fat face of Sevila, the kindly old Mexican woman who did the cooking for the ranch. Beyond these two were Jiggs, Shorty Razee, and Sundown Sloan.

One of Shorty's eyes was black and swollen shut.

"Feelin' better?" asked Buck, his drawl quiet and gentle.

Donna nodded painfully. "My throat," she murmured thickly. "Wh- . . . what happened?"

"Don't worry a bit about anythin'," Buck said soothingly. "Try and get some sleep." He patted Donna's hand and then addressed the others. "Sevila, give her a hot bath and put her to bed. She'll be fit enough by daylight. C'mon, boys . . . let's get some rest ourselves. There's plenty of work ahead for us."

They trooped out, leaving her alone with Sevila,

who hovered over her with gentle solicitude, murmuring guttural phrases of endearment.

In her strong arms she helped Donna to a tub of hot water, almost carrying her, and ministered to her much as if she were a child. The bath was wonderfully revivifying and, of a sudden, Donna remembered everything.

"Sevila!" she cried. "Does he hate me . . . does Buck hate me . . . for letting Cur- . . . that . . . that man get away? What a fool I am . . . what a fool."

She began to sob and Sevila crooned softly to her.

"There . . . there, *querida*. It ees all right. And no . . . *Señor* Buck he would not hate you. In hees own arms did he carry you here. And he hold you tight . . . oh, so very tight . . . and hees face was so gray and unhappy until he see that you was not so bad hurt. One thing eet ees certain though . . . there will be a vengeance done for thees. When *Señor* Buck see those marks on your throat, hees eyes were terrible. There was death in them. I . . . Sevila see that."

Wisely, Sevila let Donna have her spell of tears, then she slowly tucked her into bed.

"Think no more of anytheeng, *querida mia*," she comforted Donna. "Sleep, for eet will make you strong and well."

The soporific effect of the whiskey and hot bath soon made itself felt. Besides, Donna felt emotionally exhausted. She was soon sound asleep, and color crept back into her wan cheeks.

It was still an hour before dawn. The world was chill and stark and somnolent. In the vault of the heavens the stars were beginning to slowly fade. Along the eastern horizon a thread of silver pierced the sky.

Horses snorted gustily as they trooped the length of Cedarville. They stamped to a halt before the little shack, which at one and the same time composed Sheriff Jack Carleton's office and sleeping quarters.

Buck English swung stiffly from the saddle and pounded on the door.

Presently a sound of movement came from within and the door swung open, to disclose Jack Carleton in undershirt and overalls. He was yawning and his eyes were heavy with sleep. At sight of his visitor however, the sheriff snapped wide awake.

"Buck!" he exclaimed. "What's wrong? C'mon in . . . all you boys. Somebody rustle a fire in that stove while I get my boots on."

When he returned, he found Buck and the others crowded about the stove, for the dawn hours of the desert and mesa are chilly.

"Well?" he asked quietly.

Buck spoke swiftly. "Yesterday . . . at dusk . . . Curly Whipple tried to dry-gulch me, Jack. He missed me and creased Red Scudder. Red's makin' the grade without much trouble. We caught Whipple and took him out to the ranch. We locked him in the saddle shed where I had Jiggs and Shorty guardin' him for the night. I figured on puttin' the pressure on him this mornin' and makin' him talk and tell me who put him up to the idea of taking me out.

"But Miss Donna . . . her and Whipple been pretty good friends, y'know . . . well, she figured maybe there had been a mistake or a misunderstanding somewhere, which was only natural on her part. So she went down and made Jiggs and Shorty let her in to have a talk with Whipple. I reckon she found out the kind of snake he is. Anyway . . . he choked her some and made a break for it. He got away in the dark.

"Miss Donna's all right now. Scared her more than anythin', I reckon. So me and the boys came on in to tell you that from here on out, we're packin' our guns, sittin' light in the leather and tied down. Somethin' mighty dirty is in the wind and we don't figure to get caught unawares again. What's your say on the thing?"

Carleton digested the news in frowning silence. When he looked up, his eyes were hard as flint.

"My ideas are the same as yours, Buck," he said harshly. "No man can be blamed for throwin' lead in defense of his life and property. They're forcin' this on us. We'll . . ."

161

"*They* . . . Jack?" interrupted Buck. "Who do you mean by . . . they?"

"Canole, Slonicker . . . and Daggett," snapped Carleton. "You see . . . yesterday after you and Red left with those two new riders, one of the boys who owes me a favor came here and told me that Canole, Slonicker, and Daggett . . . along with Curly Whipple, put in quite a session of talk in the back room of the Silver King.

"He also informed me that Whipple pulled out along the mesa trail ahead of you fellows. And then, after Whipple had left, Daggett called in Buzz Layton and Pete Vanalia.

"That back-room confab didn't break up for two hours. Now Daggett may figure I'm a fool. And mebbe I am in some ways. But he ain't pullin' the wool over my eyes no more. Him and Canole and Slonicker are out to break me . . . one way or another. Sittin' tight and playin' politics ain't gonna help me. Sooner or later I'll lose this office anyhow, and by that time . . . unless I take a stand . . . I won't have no ranch left to go home to.

"So from here on out I fight 'em . . . straight up and down. Yeah . . . you boys should be packing guns . . . and you use 'em if you have to. If Daggett tries to put the screws on me about this job, I'll smash his pug-ugly face clear back between his ears. My term is good for two years yet and while it lasts I aim to be sheriff . . . plenty."

Buck smiled grimly. "That's the talk, Jack. It'll make things a heap simpler. For the present, just sit tight and say nothin'. But when I yell, come a-runnin' . . . ready to do some arrestin'. If they make any more talk about your usin' the office to further your own ends . . . we'll call on 'em to prove it. Somethin' tells me they won't want too strict an investigation to take place." He turned to the others. "Boys . . . you got your orders. Don't go outta your way to start anythin' with the S C Connected. But if they start it . . . finish it for 'em right on the spot. Now let's be gettin' home. I got a hunch I want to work some on."

Donna Carleton slept until nearly noon.

She dressed and breakfasted and went outside. She spied Sundown Sloan puttering with a hinge on one of the corral gates.

"Hello, Sundown," she said huskily. "Have you seen Buck . . . Mister English around?"

Sundown nodded. "Reckon you might find him down by the Gold Spring, honey. He was headin' that way about fifteen minutes ago. How you feelin' this mornin'?"

"Thanks. Oh . . . I'm all right . . . but not exactly proud of myself."

Sundown grinned. "Shucks! Don't go to feelin' that way, child. Nobody is blamin' you."

"I'll feel better when I am sure of that," murmured Donna to herself as she moved away.

"A lot better." She headed where Sundown had directed her.

She saw Buck standing beside the basin of the spring, his head bent in thought. He showed traces of his sleepless night. His eyes were slightly sunken and there were lines about his tight-clipped mouth.

At sight of Donna, he nodded quietly. " 'Mornin', Miss Donna," he drawled. "Feelin' better?"

"Not too well," she said bravely. "I just wanted you to know that I'm not a bit proud of my judgment. It was entirely wrong. And . . . I'm sorry about being responsible for letting Whipple get away. It was all my fault."

Buck studied her intently, then smiled, his face lighting up and his eyes becoming warm. "Spoken like a little thoroughbred. Now . . . knowin' what I do, I'm just as well satisfied that he did make an escape."

Donna eyed him doubtfully. "You're just saying that," she accused. "You think it will make me feel better."

"If it does . . . I'm plumb tickled. But I mean it . . . just the same. And probably for reasons you'd never guess."

"What are they?" she asked.

"Well, you see, Whipple never stopped for a horse or nothin'. He just piled right out afoot and hid somewhere in the dark. This mornin' I went over his ridin' outfit. There was a pair of saddlebags tied to his hull. They were empty . . . but I looked 'em over just the same. And what do you think I found sifted down into the seams of one of 'em?"

Donna was frankly puzzled. "I can't imagine. What?"

"Arsenic powder," Buck said slowly. "And this was the spring he poisoned with it . . . either him . . . or Buzz Layton and Pete Vanalia."

Donna was astounded. "You . . . you mean that all the while he was visiting me he was . . . ?"

"Exactly, Miss Donna. It sure shapes up that way to me. On the face of it, it looks like Layton and Vanalia were drawin' double wages all the time they been here. From your uncle . . . and from the S C Connected. Tell me . . . do you ever recollect Whipple doin' much talkin' with either of them two while he was comin' and goin' around the ranch here?"

"Why . . . yes . . . now that you mention it . . . I recall that he did. He generally managed to do a little chatting with one or the other of them. I remember asking him one time if he had known them before they came here." She paused to think for several seconds, then blurted out: "And . . . oh, Buck . . . it was Whipple who recommended them for jobs to Uncle Jack."

"Sure"—Buck nodded—"the tumblers are clickin' into place. I reckon my hunch was good in sendin' Jiggs and Shorty on a trip into the Kanab Basin to read a few brands."

Donna understood. "You mean the cattle we've been losing might have been driven into the basin?"

"I'm guessin' so."

They were silent a moment. Donna took her courage into her hands. "Tell me," she asked, "why were you and Whipple enemies before either of you ever came here? And why have you intimated that he . . . he wasn't fit for me to speak to?"

Buck's eyes met hers unwaveringly. "That's somethin' we'd all better forget, Miss Donna. You know now why I said that and that Whipple truly is a sneak and a rat. Let it go at that."

She knew better than to press the point. It would avail her nothing. So she subjugated her piqued curiosity. "Very well. And thank you for being so generous about my . . . my foolishness last night."

Jack Carleton rode up to the Red Mesa Ranch shortly before noon. He went directly to the small office and found Buck just in the act of sealing a letter.

It had taken Buck a long two hours to write that letter. Several times he had started it, only to crumple the sheets and toss them into the wooden box that acted as a catch-all.

But he had finally finished it to his satisfaction.

He tucked it into an inner pocket as the sheriff stamped in.

"I'm mad, Buck," Carleton said abruptly, "and gettin' madder all the time. I've made up my mind to carry the fight right into the enemy's camp. I'm goin' after Whipple, and when I find him, I'll arrest him for attempted murder. What do you think of the scheme?"

"Great, Jack, and I got another charge to add to it." Buck went on to tell of finding the traces of arsenic powder in Whipple's saddlebags. "Also," he ended, "once we get him behind the bars there'll be another charge comin' up. I'll explain later. And, Jack, I sent Jiggs and Shorty on a trip into the Kanab Basin to look over some brands. It won't surprise me none to find some Bar C cattle that a runnin' iron had changed to an S C Connected. It'd be simple enough to run your iron into an S C Connected. Lookee here."

Buck picked up a pencil and scrawled a few marks on a piece of paper. "Run the bar along until it touches the C. Then add a curve at each end of the bar and you got it. Savvy?"

Carleton nodded, his eyes going bleak.

"I savvy, right enough. That crowd sure were makin' a merry jackass outta me. But they're all done. I'm headin' for the S C Connected right after dinner."

"It might be wise for you to have company, Jack. I'll amble along with you."

"Good. Where's Donna?"

"She was headin' into the house, last I saw of her. Well, I'm goin' over now to change the bandage on Red Scudder's head. The ole fire-eater got a dirty wallop. C'mon, and say hello."

They both disappeared into the bunkhouse.

At the same time, Donna crossed the patio to the office. Sevila had told her of her uncle's arrival, and she wanted to see him. But the office was empty and Donna was just about to leave again, when her eye caught a scrawled line or two on a crumpled sheet of paper lying beside the desk. She picked it up and straightened it out. As she read, a slow, hot color beat up into her cheeks. The words ran:

Miss Laura Kane,
Navajo Springs,
Welkin Valley, Utah

Dear Laura,
    Love gone bad is a hard thing to write about. But I owe you too much not to see that you and the baby get a square deal. I've found out . . .

It ended there, being one of the sheets Buck had started his letter on, then discarded.

Donna read it over twice and the crimson of

her face faded to a dead, stricken white. Her lips quivered and a hurt choked gasp broke from her lips. For a moment she sagged against the desk.

Then her head came up and her blue eyes blazed. With jerky, fumbling emphasis she tore the paper to shreds and tossed them aside.

Then she walked stiffly back to her own room, where she locked the door and flung herself on her bed.

Later, she forced herself to the dinner table, where she managed, by a strong session of will power, to seem much of her old self.

However, when Buck addressed a remark to her, she favored him with a curt answer and a glance of such searing, blazing scorn and contempt that it left him completely bewildered and chilled.

He withdrew into a shell of silence and absorbed himself with his food.

Immediately after the meal, he and the sheriff took the trail for the S C Connected Ranch.

The S C Connected showed none of the industry and thriftiness of the Red Mesa Ranch. The buildings were cheaply put up, unpainted, and weather-worn. The corrals sagged dispiritedly and many rails were missing. The main ranch house was a two-storied affair, roughly built with a single upstairs window looking down above the narrow porch.

When Buck and Sheriff Jack Carleton rode up, they thought the place was deserted. But as they reined in and dismounted before the house, Monk Canole waddled out to the porch, followed by Wolf Slonicker. Canole's simian features drew into a taunting grin.

"Well, well," he growled. "This is an honor. A visit from a neighbor and a friend . . . a very old and well-known friend."

Buck's eyes glinted icily. "Wrong, Canole," he grated. "I pick my friends more careful than that."

Canole's grin changed to a snarl. "What's on your minds?"

Carleton answered. "I'm lookin' for Curly Whipple. If he's around here, trot him out. I'm arrestin' him."

"Arrestin' him!" exclaimed Canole with mock surprise. "What you arrestin' Curly for? He ain't broke no law."

"If he hasn't, he'll have his chance to prove it," said Carleton quietly. "I want him. Where is he?"

"Well, that's just too bad," broke in Slonicker's nasal voice. "He ain't here. We don't know where he is. He ain't been around for a couple of days."

"Sorry I can't take your word for that, Slonicker," stated the sheriff. "I aim to look the premises over."

"Where's your search warrant?" blurted Canole. Jack Carleton drew himself up very straight and his glance was flinty. He patted first his badge of office—then the gun hanging at his waist.

"These are good enough warrants for me, Canole. C'mon, Buck . . . we'll tackle the house first."

Things happened then, with thunderous rapidity. Buck never knew what it was that caused him to flash a glance upward toward that lone window above the porch. Perhaps it was some sixth sense, some instinct of perpetual watchfulness that had been inculcated in him through years of training and experience. At any rate, he did look up, straight into the muzzle of a Winchester, behind which were the narrowed eyes and snarl-twisted face of Curly Whipple.

Buck's subsequent actions were purely reflex. He dropped to his knees beneath a slashing slug that jerked his hat as it passed. His own guns seemed to fairly leap from the holsters to his hands, and he blasted two shots in return, fired so close together that the reports blended in a single heavy cough.

The Winchester tipped out of the window and clattered on the low roof of the porch. Whipple toppled back from sight, his left shoulder limp and twitching.

Jack Carleton had not been far behind Buck in action. His gun was out and couched at his hip, the steady muzzle taking in Canole and Slonicker. It looked like Canole was about to draw.

"Steady!" barked Carleton. "Steady!"

Then he staggered—and a gun bellowed from off to one side. Buck had come to his feet, crouching—and he swung to face this new threat.

He saw Buzz Layton and Pete Vanalia advancing slowly from one of the outbuildings. Perhaps twenty yards separated them and they were shooting steadily.

Lead hissed and ripped about Buck and Carleton, hungry—life-seeking. There was no mercy in Buck's icy, unwinking gaze. He went into action with a speed that blurred the reports of his guns to a chopping, unbroken roll.

Layton was the first to go down, his arms thrown toward the sky before he toppled forward. Vanalia was harder to stop. Buck knew that his lead was going home. In fact, twice he saw gouts of dust jump from Vanalia's shirt as the bullets struck. Yet the man seemed galvanized by some terrible hate that would not let him die. But though he kept his feet momentarily, his lead was flying wild and erratic. Then his eyes went slowly vacuous, his head dropped, and he crumpled down in a motionless heap.

Buck whirled to face Canole and Slonicker. From the corner of his eye he saw that Carleton was weaving drunkenly, though his gun still bore on the two renegade ranch owners.

"Take it easy, Jack," Buck advised, his voice cracking. "I'm watchin' these two now."

As though Buck's voice had severed some supporting fiber, Sheriff Jack Carleton sighed and toppled over.

Meeting Buck's eyes, Canole and Slonicker went white and shaken. Canole licked his lips. His hands went up and he fell back a step.

"Don't . . . don't shoot," he gasped. "We quit . . . we quit."

For a moment things hung in a balance. Buck's eyes were scorching—filmed with cold fire. His hooked thumbs curled about the hammer spurs of his guns, drawing them back—poised—ready.

Canole spoke again, his words a mere whisper. "I tell you we quit. Gawd! Don't shoot!"

Buck shook his head, as though to clear it of some gruesome mist. Slowly he relaxed.

"Unbuckle those gun belts and let 'em drop," he said, "an' watch your hands. You're dancin' on the edge of hell right now . . . and it's yawnin' for you. Quick! Do it!"

The buckles were ripped open and the guns thudded to the porch floor.

"Now back up . . . against that wall . . . and put your hands high . . . high!"

The order was obeyed as quickly and implicitly as the others.

Buck stepped over beside Carleton and dropped on one knee. He holstered his left-hand gun, then fumbled with his free hand until it rested over Carleton's heart. Relief shone in his eyes.

Carleton was alive, his heart beating steady and strong.

"Canole," snapped Buck. "Come here. Tell me where he's hurt . . . and how bad. Quick!"

Buck stepped aside, keeping his eyes on both of the renegades.

Kneeling at Carlton's side, Canole reported: "In the chest . . . pretty high up. Bullet went clear through. Serious . . . but not necessarily fatal."

Buck nodded.

"Slonicker, go upstairs and bring Whipple down. I'm countin' sixty. If you ain't back by that time . . . or if you try some kind of a break, I'm wipin' out Canole right where he stands. That's gospel. Get goin'."

Slonicker nodded, and went into the house.

In half the specified time he was back, with Whipple draped over his shoulder.

"Is he dead?" snapped Buck.

"No. Just gone under. His shoulder is smashed up pretty bad."

"Okay. Now get water and bandages. Remember . . . Canole pays if you slip."

Slonicker made no slip. He was muttering to himself: "What a tiger. Gawd, what a tiger."

While Buck watched, Carleton and Whipple were laid on the porch and their wounds washed and bandaged. When the job was done, Buck nodded.

"I see a buckboard down by the corrals.

Slonicker, go harness some horses to it. We're headin' for Cedarville with these two men. Hurry up. Canole . . . you stay put. You're still my hostage."

Monk Canole sweat blood for ten long minutes. Though a partner of his, Slonicker was no model of honor and virtue to Canole, and there was nothing to keep Slonicker from jumping a horse and tearing out. Buck could not leave and Slonicker could have made a getaway. And Canole knew that he would pay—just as Buck had promised. There was no mercy in this icy-eyed terror. But Canole's fears were groundless. Evidently Slonicker was too stunned—too completely cowed for the moment to pull any act of treachery. He soon came back, driving the buckboard.

Blankets were piled thickly in the back of the conveyance. Carleton and Whipple were lifted in, side by side. Then, with Canole and Slonicker in the seat, the rig started for Cedarville.

Buck brought up the rear in the saddle, watchful, ever alert, and leading Jack Carleton's horse.

VII

A handy rider brought word to Donna of what
had happened. In reply she covered the distance
between the ranch and town faster than she had
ever traveled it before.

When she arrived in Cedarville, Buck met
her at the door of Carleton's office, grave and
reserved and still of face.

"Jack'll make out all right," he answered to her
first incoherent question. "The doctor has just
finished with him. But he can't be disturbed at
present. He's sleepin'."

Donna insisted on seeing her uncle with her
own eyes, then obediently left the room where
the wounded man lay.

Now she faced Buck across the office.

"How did it happen and who did it?" she
demanded.

Buck explained briefly. "Either Layton or
Vanalia got Jack," he ended.

"And . . . and you killed . . . Layton and
Vanalia?" she whispered thickly, unconsciously
recoiling a step, while her eyes went to Buck's
lean hands that were deftly rolling a cigarette. It
was as though she expected to see them bathed in
crimson.

Buck did not miss the significance of her actions. But his expression did not change.

"Yeah," he answered. "I killed 'em. I tried to rock off Whipple, too . . . but it was a snap shot and I just crippled his shoulder. They tag me as a . . . a killer. I reckon I am. But . . . I reckon even a killer has his uses. Your uncle wouldn't be alive right now . . . if I hadn't been with him."

Donna would have answered, but an interruption came.

Curt Daggett walked in the door, his crafty lips twined about a black stogy. He was puffing at it nervously.

"What's all this foolishness I hear about Canole and Slonicker and Whipple being locked up?" he demanded.

"They are," answered Buck crisply.

"Under what authority?"

"This." Buck tapped one gun.

"And where . . . may I ask . . . do you fit into the picture?" rasped Daggett, in bare sarcasm.

"Just where I stand, Daggett. I'm runnin' Jack Carleton's affairs until he's well enough to run 'em himself. Furthermore . . . you keep that long nose of yours out of 'em. I've heard all about you. As far as I can see there ain't a bit of lily polish anywhere on you. My straight opinion is . . . you ought to be in the lock-up yourself. And unless you watch your step, I'll put you there."

Daggett's laugh was a trifle forced. "That's pretty high-handed talk, young fellow."

"I'll make it stick. If you think I'm wrong . . . the next move is up to you. Make your bluff stand . . . or shut up. I'm not much of a hand at law. To me it's good only as long as it works in the right direction. When it doesn't . . . I pass it by. You can't bluff me."

"But you can't keep those men in jail. They've . . ."

"I'm keepin' them there, just the same," broke in Buck curtly. "Now save your breath. You can't get 'em out and you can't go in and talk to 'em. In fact . . . you can't do a thing but get out of here and mind your own business. I'm dead for sleep. Be on your way."

Daggett was fairly shivering with rage, but he left the office.

Buck turned to Donna. "What I told him about needin' sleep was true," he said gruffly—but not without gentleness. "If you'll excuse me, I'm curlin' up on that bunk in the corner and catchin' some shut-eye. You best go over to the hotel and get yourself a room for the night. I'll make sure the doctor keeps you posted about any changes in Jack."

For a moment the haggard weariness of his face almost softened Donna. She was on the verge of kinder words. But she caught herself, nodded, and left.

178

It was dark when Buck awoke. He sat up abruptly, as though some foreign sound had broken his slumber. For a long moment he listened. The only echo that came to his ears was the rapidly diminishing cadence of swiftly moving hoofs on the street outside. Some cowpunchers probably, on their way back home.

He started to lie down again, but that queer sense of something wrong pulled him upright once more.

He rolled and lit a cigarette, inhaled a moment, then shrugged and got to his feet. He tiptoed to the rear quarters of the office and looked in. The doctor and Donna were there, bending over Jack Carleton.

Donna looked up, and shook her head at the gleam of alarm in Buck's eyes.

"We're just checking up," she whispered. "He's doing splendidly."

Buck nodded and closed the door. He went to the front portal and threw it open, looking out upon the dark world. Still that feeling of something being wrong plagued him. He thought suddenly of his prisoners.

Striding quickly over to the jail, he unlocked the door and opened it.

"Everything all right in here?" he barked.

There was no answer. Buck drew a gun with one hand and lit a match with the other. As the meager light flared he stared around. A low curse broke from his lips. There was but one man in that jail where there should have been three.

This one was Curly Whipple, stretched flat on his back on one of the bunks. And a heavy-hafted Bowie knife was buried to the hilt in his breast.

A single glance showed that Whipple was dead. Buck turned away, scratching another match.

The means of Canole and Slonicker's escape was plain. The bars of the window had been cut, evidently with a hack-saw.

Buck left the jail, locking the door behind him. His eyes were narrowed, his face grim. The job wasn't finished yet. A lot of it had to be done all over again. But he knew there was nothing to do but wait until morning, for pursuit now, in the darkness, would be useless. He went back to the office to get some more sleep for the work to be done in the days ahead.

The pursuit did not start, however, for three days. Jack Carleton did not rally as fast as expected and Buck would not leave until he knew the sheriff was out of danger and until he had had a talk with him.

It was three days later that the doctor said that finally Buck might discuss matters with Carleton.

Carleton's face was thin and his eyes sunken. But he was better and his head appeared to be clear. The doctor left the two of them alone.

"I'll do most of the talkin', Jack," Buck advised him. "You listen, and if my plan seems sound, nod your head. In the first place, Canole and Slonicker broke jail. They had outside help. It looks like Daggett's work to me. I aim to prove that later.

"But before they took off from the jail, they left a knife stuck in Whipple. As I see it . . . they knew he couldn't run with them in the condition he was, and they was afraid of what he might tell us. So they killed him before slopin'. That was murder. I'm goin' after 'em. Where they went . . . I don't know. But I'll get 'em, if it takes ten years. I'm pinnin' a deputy's badge on myself. Do you agree?"

Carleton nodded. "Yeah," he whispered weakly. "I'm authorizin' you to get 'em, Buck. Don't take no chances with polecats like them. If they don't cave quick, lad . . . go a-shootin'. And good luck."

Buck leaned down and pressed the sheriff's hand. "I'll be seein' you, Jack. Just concentrate on gettin' well. Don't worry. *Adiós*."

Buck went back to the office and made his preparations. He got a scabbarded Winchester from the office storeroom, cleaned and oiled it, and stuffed several boxes of ammunition into a pair of saddlebags.

From one drawer of the battered desk he

181

unearthed a deputy's badge and pinned it on the breast pocket of his shirt. Then he gathered up the equipment and went out.

Donna was just coming from the hotel. Buck had already told her of Slonicker and Canole's escape—as well as the fate of Curly Whipple. She was pale and distressed looking.

"You're going after . . . those two?" she asked.

Buck nodded. "Yeah. Your uncle authorizes me to."

"There will be more bloodshed?"

"If they don't give in quiet . . . there will be."

His eyes were cool and steady and there was a relentless set to his jaw.

"There's nothin' else to be done, you see. When men rob and kill they don't deserve any consideration. They destroy others . . . well, they oughta be caught at any cost and made to pay the penalty for their crimes."

Donna was silent, so he added: "They don't rate bein' called men . . . killers like Slonicker and Canole. They've outlawed themselves. It ain't revenge I'm workin' for, it's justice. And if they come in peaceable with me, I won't have to do any shootin' . . . any killin'."

When Donna finally spoke, her voice was strained. "How . . . how long will this sort of thing keep up . . . this killing?" She got the last word out with a little shudder.

"As long as men are what they are, I reckon."

"I mean . . . with you?"

Buck shrugged. "That's a question I don't have an answer for. But don't think I enjoy it. Mostly . . . well, it just has to be done, and it seems like I been kinda elected to do it . . . lately. I'll give 'em every chance to come back in quietly."

He would have passed on, but she laid a timid hand on his arm. "Uncle Jack thinks a lot of you. Don't take any chances . . . please."

Buck looked at her long and inscrutably. He laughed a little harshly. "Thanks . . . I won't. *¡Hasta la vista!*"

He stalked off toward the livery stable, a stern, dark figure, bearing the balance of wayward men's lives in his cold, deadly courage—in the wizardry of his muscular, brown hands.

Donna watched him and tears veiled her eyes.

"Buck," she murmured softly. "Buck . . . be careful. For Uncle Jack . . . and for me, too."

At the stable Buck looked over the sheriff's string of horses and picked out a chunky, square-built roan—a mean-looking brute with a hammer head and rolling eyes. But there was endurance and bottom in every line of the horse.

Next Buck hung his scabbarded rifle under the left stirrup leather and tied the saddlebags behind the cantle. Then he mounted and swung out in to the street.

Two dusty, travel-worn cowpunchers came

swinging into view. They were Jiggs Maloney and Shorty Razee.

At sight of Buck they reined in thankfully.

"Hopin' to find you, Buck," panted Shorty. "Your hunch was right. There's plenty of cattle in the Kanab Basin country that used to be the Red Mesa's Bar C stuff. Most of 'em have got our iron run over into the S C Connected. But the dirty buzzards were mighty certain of themselves.

"A lot of the stuff was just vented . . . they was that sure of not bein' checked up on. No wonder Daggett didn't want Jack to get very far from his office. He knew that if Jack ever rode down into the Kanab Basin, he'd find out plenty. We killed one critter and skinned off the brand, just as proof. Jiggs, where's that hunk of hide?"

Jiggs produced it, and Buck studied it with narrowed eyes. He nodded.

"Good work, boys. This just about cinches matters. There's been things happenin' since you were gone. Jack was wounded, but he's doin' better now and he just needs rest. You can get the whole story from Miss Donna. Keep that piece of hide safe. I got a job ahead. I don't know when it'll be finished. Tomorrow, after you two talk to Miss Donna, you get out to the ranch. Tell Red he's foreman till I get back. Tell him to keep things movin'. I'll be seein' you."

Jiggs was struck with an afterthought. "We

see'd Slonicker and Canole ridin' into the basin, Buck. Shorty and me was out there breathin' our horses in a little gully just off the trail. Those two didn't see us, but we recognized them. The spalpeens seemed in one devil of a hurry."

Buck's eyes gleamed. "That's the best news of all, Jiggs. Much obliged. ¡*Adiós*!"

VIII

Two days later a tall, auburn-haired woman rode into Cedarville on the evening stage. She had a sweet mouth, the expression of which was belied by a veil of bitterness in her eyes. She registered at the hotel, then went directly to the sheriff's office.

Donna was there, having just left her uncle in a restful sleep.

"How do you do," said the new arrival. "Could you tell me where I might find Sheriff Carleton?"

"I'm sorry," answered Donna. "My uncle is not well. He was wounded the other day while arresting a man. He is sleeping just now. Is there any way I could help you?"

The woman hesitated. "Is there a man named Buck English around?"

Donna felt her heart go cold.

"He . . . he isn't here now. He is a deputy of, my uncle's and is out after a couple of escaped prisoners. When he returns . . . who shall I tell him was asking for him?"

"I am Laura Kane. He wrote me a few days ago, telling me to come here . . . that he had some vital information for me. Perhaps you could tell me if he was right. Is there a rider named Whipple in this vicinity . . . Curly Whipple?"

Donna gulped and felt the room spinning. Finally she stammered: "There . . . there was. He . . . he is dead . . . now."

Laura Kane took a backward step, her hands going to her throat. "Dead? Curly Whipple . . . dead? Did . . . did Buck kill him?"

She had turned pale and her eyes were wide and stricken.

Donna, recovering some of her poise, jumped up and held out a chair.

"No," she answered once she had Laura Kane settled comfortably in the chair. "Buck did not kill him. He was murdered by the men Buck is out after."

Laura Kane sank deeper into the chair. Tears trickled down her cheeks.

Donna felt a swift rush of pity. "Tell me . . . please, Miss Kane. Perhaps I can help."

Laura Kane shrugged wearily. "There isn't a great deal to tell. You see . . . I used to be Curly Whipple's wife. He . . . he deserted me and our baby . . . over a year ago. I sued for a divorce and resumed my maiden name. When . . . when

Curly and I were married . . . I signed over half my ranch to him.

"After he left me . . . I wanted to get out of the country. I have a brother . . . Johnny . . . who is in the Texas Rangers. He wants me and my child to come and live with him in Texas. I have a buyer for the ranch, but I could not sell until I had reached some kind of an understanding with Curly. Buck wrote that Curly was around here. So I came right up. Now . . . now he's dead."

Donna did not say anything. There was nothing she could say. All of the sympathy in her generous nature flowed out to this woman in distress. At the same time a tremendous, surging relief engulfed her. That letter—that fragment she had read—she understood it now—and it was as if the weight of the world had lifted from her shoulders.

Impulsively she went to Laura Kane and put her arms about her.

"When Buck comes back . . . I'm sure he will help you make matters right. Until then . . . I want to be your friend. You must come out and stay at the ranch with me. I don't know that much about legal things except that they can take so much time. Besides, you'll be lonely here in town. Will you come?"

Laura nodded. "Yes . . . and thank you. You are very kind. I . . . I haven't many friends. Buck is one of the oldest and most valued. You see,

Buck and my brother Johnny used to be the best of friends. They were inseparable. When Johnny went into the Rangers he wanted Buck to join up with him. But Buck wouldn't go. He's different . . . somehow. He's wild and splendid. Authority from others irks him. He prefers to travel his own trail in his own way. But no brother could be kinder and more gentle than Buck has been to me." She paused as if to catch her breath. Then she added: "Yes . . . I will go out to your ranch."

Donna fairly outdid herself in her hospitality to Laura Kane. The Red Mesa Ranch was quiet and when Donna had circulated the story of her guest, the ranch hands were friendly and sympathetic. Red Scudder became particularly attentive to Laura Kane, a development that Donna observed with great enthusiasm.

At the same time, there were moments when Donna was very grave, her eyes shadowed and thoughtful. She spent a lot of her time down at the mesa rim, looking out across the desert. She grew watchful—always listening—as though she were expecting someone to ride in, and, as the days moved by into a week, she became nervous and apprehensive. She fought a losing fight, and one night, in the privacy of her own room, she buried her face in a pillow and sobbed with abandon.

"Buck!" she cried. "Buck . . . come back to me!"

IX

The town of Washoe was a crude, mean, vicious little corner of iniquity, standing beside a lonely road, far to the southeast corner of Kanab Basin. Its inhabitants were furtive—watchful. Its business was merely the serving of doubtful pleasures to roistering riders who rode in from the wild reaches of the country around.

It was evening when Buck English rode into the place. For seventy long miles he had been traveling slowly, patiently, and tirelessly, following the trail of Slonicker and Canole.

It had not been an easy job, for various inhabitants of the basin had looked askance upon him for his questions and cold purpose. There were many men in the basin who had no friendship for the law and what verged closely on being an outlaw brotherhood existed in the place.

One way and another, however—Buck eked out hints and traces, and he felt, as he rode down the street of Washoe, that he had run his quarry to earth. He did not advertise his presence. His badge of authority was out of sight, and his dusty, unshaven appearance easily passed for that of a man on the dodge.

His first care was food and rest for his mount— then a wash and food for himself. He ate his greasy dinner in a shadowy, disreputable hash-house, where even the waiter was furtive and watchful.

Full-fed, Buck rolled a cigarette and looked the town over. The biggest building in it was one that housed a saloon and gambling den. Also, there was a dance hall adjacent, where painted, dead-eyed women preyed on drink-befuddled riders.

The windows of the place were thick with dirt and cobwebs, but Buck managed, by a little judicious sleuthing to get a look into the place. Almost immediately his face expressed satisfaction. In the gambling den, with three other men, were Wolf Slonicker and Monk Canole, sitting at a card table.

Buck turned back to the edge of the splintery board sidewalk and smoked his cigarette to the last ash. He tossed the butt aside, brought forth his badge of authority, and repinned it on his shirt. He drew his guns from their holsters and spun the cylinders, then replaced them.

For a long time he looked away through the night toward the northwest, to where Donna Carleton lay sobbing on her pillow. Then his head came up and his shoulders squared. As he turned toward the door of the place a shaft of light struck his face, showing it to be set and implacable. Swiftly he stalked inside.

A low gasp, then a dead silence greeted his appearance. Buck moved down one side of the room, with the wall at his back. Slonicker and Canole had not looked up. All their thought and interest was on the card game. Arriving opposite them, some ten paces away, Buck stopped and hooked his thumbs in his gun belt. His voice sounded with low, piercing intensity.

"Slonicker . . . Canole . . . I want you!"

The heads of the renegades snapped up, and their eyes met his.

Slonicker went gray.

Canole licked his lips. "Buck English!" he croaked. "Buck English!"

"And the law!" snapped Buck. "You're under arrest, you two . . . for the murder of Curly Whipple. Reach high!"

Their hands rose slowly, as they kneed their way back from the table. They stood up. Slonicker was motionless. Canole was teetering back and forth on his toes. It was plain that the ape-like renegade was working out a decision in that feral skull of his.

Buck sensed it and cautioned him with a snapping command.

"Don't try it, Canole. Your life . . . don't try it. . . ."

The rest of his words were drowned in the blur of curses that spouted from Canole's lips. The man had gone berserk from hate and fear. He snatched at his guns, lunging to one side as he did so.

Buck's hands flickered and his first slug caught Canole in the very act of the monkey-like leap. The murderer coughed and staggered, but held his feet. His guns were out, almost level. Buck's guns blared and blared again. At each impact of lead Canole staggered farther and farther backward. A loose chair interrupted his progress. He stumbled, sat down in it. The curses caught in his throat and he toppled to the floor.

As Canole fell, Slonicker made his gamble. He dropped on his knees behind the card table, from which the other players had scattered like frightened quail. His first shot spun Buck's hat from his head. Then Buck fired, and Slonicker died as he was thumbing the hammer for a second shot. His narrow head jerked back, a blue-edged hole just above one eye. He fell.

From his crouch, Buck looked around the room. "I gave 'em their chance," he said wearily. "Looks like I ride alone."

Curt Daggett sat by himself in the back room of the Silver King saloon. There was a curious pallor about his thin, slit-mouthed face. His pale eyes were more shifty than ever. He was plainly a man heavily besieged by trepidation and mental unrest. A glass and whiskey bottle were on the table before him and from time to time he poured himself a stiff drink and gulped it down.

It was midmorning, and the sun lay warm along

the street outside. A weary horse and rider came jogging in to Cedarville. The roan was gaunt and high of flank and his eyes no longer rolled. Buck English was as weary and worn as his mount, but there was a determined, implacable set to his jaw.

He reined in before the Silver King and dismounted stiffly.

Stalking through the door of the saloon, he accosted the bartender. "Daggett around?"

The bartender started to give a glib, evasive answer, but something he saw in Buck's eyes caused him to gulp and nod emphatically. "In . . . in the back room," he stuttered.

Without knocking, Buck swung open the designated door and stepped through.

Daggett started—then sat as still as a graven statue.

Buck kicked up a chair and sat down.

"We're talkin' turkey, Daggett . . . just you and me," he said abruptly. "First . . . Slonicker and Canole are dead. I caught up with 'em . . . tried to arrest 'em . . . but they took their chance. It didn't pan out for either one. Your gang is pretty badly thinned, Daggett. You're the only one amountin' to much that's left . . . and you're leavin'."

Daggett poured and gulped another drink. "What . . . what do you mean . . . I'm leavin'?"

"Just that, Daggett," Buck replied. "This neck of the woods can get along very well without you. You're lucky. The men who worked for you

got nothin' as a reward but death. But you lose
. . . just the same. I'm givin' you just five hours to
pack up and ride out of here. If you're not gone
by that time . . . well, there may very well be a
lynchin' bee. Savvy?"

Under the burn of the liquor Daggett got hold
of a few fragments of courage. "You're crazy,"
he scoffed. "You've got nothing on me. I am not
responsible for anything Slonicker and Canole
might have done."

Buck shrugged. "Your line of thought is easy
to read, Daggett. You figure with Slonicker and
Canole and Whipple dead, there isn't any danger
of them talkin' about your part in this. The same
goes for Buzz Layton and Pete Vanalia.

"But I know for a fact that them fellows were
workin' for you. Therefore, it must've been
at your orders that they rustled Red Mesa's
Bar C stock . . . that they poisoned the spring out
at the ranch . . . that Whipple tried to dry-gulch
me."

"You're crazy," parroted Daggett again, but his
hands were twitching. "I tell you I had nothing to
do with that crowd."

"You're a liar by trade," drawled Buck, "but a
danged poor one just the same. You see, Daggett
. . . before I left the Kanab Basin, I did some
prowlin' around and askin' questions. Strange
as it may seem, I found a couple of honest
ranchers down there. They admitted buyin' a

lot of Bar C stock, vented to the S C Connected brand, in good faith.

"Jack Carleton never sold a head of stock to the S C Connected in his life. Those cattle were stolen, as well as a lot more where the Bar C was run over into S C Connected. I've got iron bound evidence to that. Something else . . . the ranchers told me that in payment for the vented stock, they drew out checks . . . payable to Curtis Daggett."

Daggett recoiled and his lips sagged.

"Your bein' connected with the bank, you thought you could keep those checks under cover," went on Buck. "And by raisin' a lot of yappin' around town you kept Jack Carleton close to home, so he wouldn't find out anythin'. You were sore at him for havin' beatin' you in the election and you were out to bust him. The scheme's backfired, Daggett."

Daggett caved. "Five hours," he gulped. "I can't settle my affairs in five hours. I have interests and responsibilities and . . ."

"If you're wise," broke in Buck drily, "if you're wise . . . your main interests will be gettin' a long way from Cedarville as fast as you can. Of course"—he shrugged—"if you want to stick around and take a chance on facin' it . . . that's your business. But in five hours . . . if you're not gone . . . I will call together a representative group of citizens and put the facts in front of 'em. I said five hours . . . and I meant it."

Daggett was like a palsied old man. "I'll go," he whispered. "I'll go."

Buck stood up and walked to the door.

He turned back to add: "You're wise. You're gettin' a better break than you deserve. Canole and Slonicker and the rest . . . bad as they were . . . were men alongside of you, Daggett. You're just a rat . . . a miserable, schemin' rat. It'd be a disgrace to kill you. Remember . . . five hours!"

The door closed behind him.

Out on the Red Mesa Ranch, Donna and Laura Kane were down at the rim, gazing into the mysterious desert. Laura was flushed, her eyes shining. Yet there was a shyness, a reluctance there also—almost timidity.

Donna was unconscious of her companion's mood. Her eyes, fixed steadily upon that remote rim of the world, which was the Madrigals, were brooding and wistful and lonely. Her fine brow was puckered with worry, and the tired lines of fearful waiting were about her lips. Her thoughts, her heart, and her hopes were plainly far away, riding the trail of danger and duty with Buck English.

Abruptly Laura turned on Donna and caught both of the latter's hands.

"I don't want you to think me a silly, frivolous woman, Donna!" she exclaimed. "And if it seems strange to you, remember . . . I ceased to love

Curly Whipple many months ago. But the truth of it is, I've a secret I can't keep to myself any longer. I've got to confide in someone . . . and I hope you will be patient with me. Dear girl . . . I'm in love again."

Donna turned to her slowly, her heart writhing as though before a dagger thrust. She gasped, and it was almost a cry of pain. "Not . . . not . . . ," she was stammering helplessly.

Laura spoke again swiftly. "My marriage with Curly was all a mistake. I knew it within a month after the wedding. Curly simply was not the sort of man I thought he was and I was miserable. Life with him was unbearable. He was shifty and ill-tempered, and I could never depend on him.

"We'd quarrel, and he'd go off, sulking, and send me no word. I wouldn't know where he was, or what he was doing, or when he'd be back. I was wretched day and night. But then when he did come back . . . penitent and full of promises . . . I'd give him another chance.

"I knew it was useless, but I kept hoping something would happen to change him. I loved him once, you see, and it was a long time before I could accept the fact that we meant nothing to each other. Even then I determined to play the game . . . for . . . well, when one brings children into the world, one owes them certain obligations.

"It was a dreary outlook, living with a man who I did not love and who did not love me. But

I did my best. Then Curly left and he didn't come back. There was nothing else to do but sue for a divorce. There were limits to my pride.

"Naturally, the fact of Curly's death was a terrible shock. But I've all my life left and I think . . . I'm sure . . . that I see real happiness ahead at last. Surely I cannot be blamed for welcoming the sunlight, after the shadows through which I have walked. Our lives are what we make them, and I don't believe anyone will censure me if I strike out boldly for happiness."

Donna's mind was whirling. This woman, glowing and animated, was speaking of sunlight—of happiness. Of striking out boldly for that which one desired. But where would be the sunshine for her—the happiness? Buck and Laura Kane! It was the natural thing. They had known each other for years—had been the best of friends. Buck and Laura's brother had been pals.

And Laura was attractive enough. She had looks, poise, mental brilliance. Buck had written to her, asking her to come to the Red Mesa country. And he had hounded down the man who had wronged her. Why had she not guessed this long ago? Yes, that would be it.

No doubt Buck had always loved Laura, for he was that kind of a man. A one-woman man, whose love for that woman would follow her always, no matter what the circumstance. And yet, Buck had not seen Laura since she had arrived. Still that meant little. If he had written her one letter, he could have written her many.

Donna's thoughts flashed back over certain memories of her own, memories that had grown dearer and richer with every passing hour. Memories of the pitifully few times when she and Buck had achieved something of intimacy of thought and words. At those times he had been gentle, sincere. But Donna thought she could see now that all he ever meant was merely to be kind.

In return she had flouted him, merely because of what she had guessed and guessed wrongly about that miserable fragment of a discarded letter. Well, she'd pay a lot for that misjudgment. Too much. All her life she'd remember—and feel regret. And she could say nothing, do nothing now. . . .

Suddenly she had a clear picture of Buck English silhouetted against the sunset, and something caught tight in her throat. Oh, the splendid pride and courage and fineness of him!

But he was Laura's. . . .

Laura was pressing her hands more tightly.

"You're not angry with me. Donna?" she was saying. "Please say you're not blaming me. Oh, I'll offer some sop to the conventions. I'll wait six months before marrying again. But those months stretch ahead like an eternity."

For a moment Donna knew the wild urge

to turn on Laura like a fury, to tell her that she should not have this man, this lean, silent tiger man. To tell her that Donna Carleton also had a heart and a desire for happiness, that this same Donna Carleton also intended to reach out and grasp at that happiness. But the thoroughbred strain in Donna was too strong.

By a terrific effort she composed herself and, if her face was merely white and strained, it was only the stronger testimonial to her self-control. For the heart of her was dead.

She faced Laura and even managed a ghost of a smile, a tragic, pitiful little smile.

"You have nothing to apologize for, Laura," she said. "As you say, we must make our own lives. And happiness after your sorrow and tragedy will only make it the sweeter. I . . . I know your choice is right this time. Buck . . . Buck English is . . . wonderful! We both know that."

Laura stared at her in amazement. "Buck!" she exclaimed. "Who in the world was talking of Buck? I wasn't talking about him."

Donna caught at her, almost fiercely. "You don't . . . you didn't mean that it was Buck?"

Laura laughed joyously. "Oh . . . you dear, wonderful youngster. Of course not. I'm going to marry Red Scudder!"

Then Laura's arms went around Donna, for Donna had begun to sob.

"Don't you . . . don't you," she soothed. "You

game little thoroughbred. You were willing to wish me well and all the time your heart was breaking because you thought it was Buck. Why, you and Buck were made for each other.

"Don't you think I've known all along? Well, I have. You've been worried sick about him. I've seen it in your eyes. I've heard it in your voice. But he'll come back to you, quiet, still-faced as always. I've known Buck a long, long time. He is one man who fortune loves. He laughs at danger, and, Lord knows, he whips it at every turn of the road. Hold the same faith in him that he holds in himself. He'll come back. He'll always come back."

A spur chain clashed on a rock behind them. They turned—and were rigid. A queer, whimpering cry of relief broke from Donna.

Laura was the first to recover. She jumped to her feet.

"Buck!" she cried. "Buck English."

He came slowly up and took Laura's outstretched hand.

"Sure," he drawled quietly. "I reckon you've heard?"

Laura nodded, her eyes sobering. "Yes, Buck . . . I've heard. It . . . well, those things happen in life."

"Yeah," agreed Buck. "They do. I'll get busy with a law shark and clear up the title to your ranch so you can sell out, Laura."

She shook her head, and color crept into her cheeks.

"I . . . I'm not going to sell it, Buck. Here . . . I've a secret to tell you."

She pulled his head down and whispered in his ear.

Buck grinned joyously.

"No!" he exploded. "Why, the lucky old red-headed son-of-a-gun. Wait till I get my hands on him. If I don't whale him but good! By golly . . . I'm tickled to death, Laura. Old Red's a real, four-square man. You ain't makin' no mistake this time." He hugged and patted her shoulder, saying: "Now be a good girl and run along up to the house. I've got somethin' to say . . . and it ain't for your ears."

Laura laughed and hurried away.

Buck looked at Donna.

She had turned to face the desert again. He did not know it, but she was trembling.

He drew a deep breath and stepped up beside her.

"Donna," he said quietly.

She looked up at him, color beating in her cheeks, her eyes moist. "Hello, Buck," she answered.

He seemed to be groping for his words. His hands fumbled at his waist. First one, then the other of his criss-crossed gun belts fell free. He laid them on the rock beside Donna.

"I'm wonderin' . . . wonderin' if I laid these guns away . . . if you'd look at me as somethin' different from a human wolf," he said quietly. "I used to think that I'd be plumb satisfied with life if I could do nothin' else but pack those two guns and ride lone, hard trails. But that was before I met you. I know different now. There's a new quality in the sunset . . . in the dawn . . . in the stars for me now. I've tried to think different, but it isn't any use."

His voice took on a new intensity.

"Everywhere I look . . . I see your face . . . every sound I hear is your voice. The whole world is different . . . now. I don't know a heap about this thing called love. It never entered my life before. I never knew my mother . . . she died before I was old enough to experience her love. Dad . . . well, I worshiped him. But that was the love of son for father. This other . . . it's like some glory that's grown in me, a hunger that I can't get away from. I wish I could have come to you different . . . without the stain of crimson on my hands. But that's in the past now. I'm just what I am . . . and I love you. Is there any chance for me . . . Donna?"

His eyes, anxious and pleading, rested on her face, but he could not read there the answer to his question. There was a still, brooding look about her, and he waited, not daring to speak the words that rushed up from his heart, words of longing and despair, and of a fierce exultant hope that was almost intolerable in its intensity.

She was silent so long his face became almost haggard. Slowly she stood up and turned. She picked up the belts and holsters with their deadly contents. First one, then the other she buckled into place about his waist.

Her eyes lifted to his at last.

"I wouldn't have you any different, Buck," she told him softly. "As you stand now . . . as you have always been . . . I love you!"

The sun arched and sank beyond the Madrigals. The desert softened, deepened—grew shadowy and luring. The night wind rushed upward from the gulf of the universe. Darkness grew about them. Still they sat there, she curled within the circle of his arm.

In them, and in the world about them, breathed the promise of eternity.

About the Author

L.P. Holmes was the author of a number of outstanding Western novels. Born in a snowed-in log cabin in the heart of the Rockies near Breckenridge, Colorado, Holmes moved with his family when very young to northern California and it was there that his father and older brothers built the ranch house where Holmes grew up and where, in later life, he would live again. He published his first story—"The Passing of the Ghost"—in *Action Stories* (9/25). He was paid a ½¢ a word and received a check for $40. "Yeah . . . forty bucks," he said later. "Don't laugh. In those far-off days . . . a pair of young parents with a three-year-old son could buy a lot of groceries on forty bucks." He went on to contribute nearly six hundred stories of varying lengths to the magazine market as well as to write numerous Western novels. For many years of his life, Holmes would write in the mornings and spend his afternoons calling on a group of friends in town, among them the blind Western author, Charles H. Snow, who Lew Holmes always called Judge Snow (because he was Napa's Justice of the Peace from 1920-1924) and who frequently makes an appearance in later novels as a local justice in Holmes's imaginary

Western communities. Holmes produced such notable novels as *Somewhere They Die* (1955) for which he received the Spur Award from the Western Writers of America. In his novels one finds those themes so basic to his Western fiction: the loyalty that unites one man to another, the pride one must take in his work and a job well done, the innate generosity of most of the people who live in Holmes's ambient Western communities, and the vital relationship between a man and a woman in making a better life together.

Books are produced in the United States using U.S.-based materials

Books are printed using a revolutionary new process called THINKtech™ that lowers energy usage by 70% and increases overall quality

Books are durable and flexible because of Smyth-sewing

Paper is sourced using environmentally responsible foresting methods and the paper is acid-free

Center Point Large Print
600 Brooks Road / PO Box 1
Thorndike, ME 04986-0001 USA

(207) 568-3717

US & Canada:
1 800 929-9108
www.centerpointlargeprint.com